A Dangerous Hunger

BOOK TWO

The Sentinel Demons

J. S. SCOTT

A Dangerous Hunger
The Sentinel Demons: Book Two

Copyright © 2014 by J. S. Scott

Content Editing by Roroblu's Mum
Cover Art: Cali MacKay – Covers By Cali
Copy Editing by Faith Williams – The Atwater Group

ISBN: 978-1-939962-46-1 (Paperback)
ISBN: 978-1-939962-45-4 (Digital Edition)

This book is dedicated to every wonderful member of *Jan's Gems*, my fabulous street team. I've never seen a more enthusiastic and incredible group of women, and I know I'm blessed to have every one of you in my group. Your support means the world to me. I hope you like Drew's story.

Contents

Prologue

"The Sentinel Demons-A History"
AUTHOR-UNKNOWN

Many people believe that demons are evil spirits, possessing humans, taking over their minds and bodies until they are nothing but a shell, a vessel for the evil entity that dwells inside them. What most humans don't know is that there are also other types of demons, physical beings created thousands of years ago, during a period of time when demons came to rule the Earth, having been set loose by careless gods who used them for chaos and revenge. The gods created them in so great a number that they finally had to confine all their creations to a demon realm, a prison that could contain them. Said gods, who are now considered nothing more than myth, and whose vanity was endless, adamantly refused to destroy the demons—to annihilate all of them would be an admission that what the deities had done was actually wrong. All-powerful, all-knowing gods and demigods did not make errors. They themselves declared it impossible. And how could they destroy their own magic, lose creatures that might be needed later? After all, the gods were usually at war, and what if they needed their evil creations for weapons? So instead, the demons stayed confined to the demon realm, a place where no god would venture—a realm of such vile evilness, such toxicity and so malodorous, that no selfish deity could tolerate visiting.

The realm was hidden, situated between Earth and Hades, a place where the demons remained, multiplied, and grew in strength while the gods ignored their existence. Unfortunately, ignoring such heinous immortals eventually created utter chaos, the demons finally gaining enough power to leave the demon realm and create havoc on an Earth that was, by that time, inhabited by a large population of humans. These demons became known as the Evils.

Devastation ruled, humans being taken in large numbers, disappearing in droves. The balance between good and evil tipped, evil ruling the planet, creating a rift that not even the gods themselves could fix. Desperate to restore sanity to an insane world, the gods tried in vain to destroy the vile beasts that upset the equilibrium, finally putting aside their vanity in favor of survival. But it was too late; the demon population was too large, too powerful, and the egotistic gods weren't about to venture near the Evils to destroy them.

Desperate, the deities banded together and created a new breed of demon to fight the Evils; the newcomers' souls would still be dark, but their purpose would be to protect humans from becoming extinct, bringing good and evil back into balance. These newly created Sentinel demons blended in, appearing human...but they weren't. They were magical beings, although they adapted and took on more facets of humanity as they evolved. Having given the guardian demons the power to recruit humans and thus replace Sentinels lost in the battle between good and evil, the gods no longer needed to be bothered with their "annoying little problem" and went to war with each other once again, losing power as the centuries passed and humans ceased to worship them. However, the Sentinels carried on, striving to protect the human population, governing themselves and growing in magical powers, even though the gods had embedded a set of rules into the Sentinels' magic—supposed fail-safes imposed to keep the guardian demons in check. Still, the Sentinels brought balance back to the planet in spite of the stifling rules, finding ways to bend them or work around them, angry that the only rule imposed on the Evils was that human victims could not initially be taken by force, or coerced via lies. But manipulation was easy for an Evil, and once a human had agreed to an Evil's bargain, there was no end to the torture the heinous demons could impose upon the duped individual in order to increase their own strength.

So...are all demons evil? They are all dark at their core, and have some degree of inherent wickedness...but demons were not all created equal.

Evils and Sentinels are both demons, engaging to this day in a battle of good versus evil that has been going on for thousands of years, a war that most humans are blissfully unaware even exists. However, for the small percentage of individuals who actually have encounters with demons...their lives will never be the same.

Chapter One

If there was one thing Drew Winston loved about his earthly Sentinel existence, it was food. Undoubtedly, he loved being a billionaire demon, but he mostly loved the money because it allowed him to get any type of food he wanted, whenever he wanted it, and he hadn't yet met a steak or a dessert that he didn't like. Sure, some of the food was better than others, but food was a glorious thing, and he hadn't tired of any of it during his over one hundred fifty years of being a Sentinel.

If there was one thing Drew detested about living on the planet in the human dimension, it was cats. They were nasty, sneaky animals that did nothing but hiss at him and give him the evil eye whenever he crossed their path, attacking him with claws and teeth if he got too close, so he tried to stay well away from that feline breed altogether. Cats obviously sensed his demon, and to say that they didn't react well to it was an understatement.

Given his long, unfortunate history with cats, he was a little beyond surprised when a large, orange, very overfed tabby cat made its way over to where he was sitting, curling up not five feet away from him.

"I don't like cats," he warned the feline. "And they don't like me. So scram." He waved away the animal, but the cat never flinched, and continued to give him a curious golden-eyed stare. Not the evil eye exactly, but more of an assessing glare. The cat didn't move, nor did it hiss. It just kept peering at him as though trying to figure out who he was and what he was doing in its owner's territory.

Bloody hell! was the thought that formed as Drew opened the note he'd crumpled in his hand and read it again:

Dear Demons,

I'm not home, so you might as well leave and never come back. I'm getting more than a little tired of this game, and I'm not obtuse enough to agree to any demon bargain. I'm under Sentinel protection. So take your ugly asses back to your own realm so I can get some work done. Trying to corner me and get me to agree to a bargain is pointless.

Dr. Talia Maris

Drew laughed. He couldn't help himself. He wasn't used to humans who didn't cower at the thought of demons being on their ass. This woman seemed more irritated than terrified, and that intrigued him.

However, he had to admit that his ego was getting a little bruised, too. He'd been trying to corner this human female to have a little discussion with her about her research for well over a month, and she'd outsmarted him every time. He was a Sentinel, and he never failed to do his duty, and being bested by a human female was getting beyond annoying.

"She's a smart lass, isn't she?" he asked aloud, glancing at the cat. The feline tilted its head, as though to say that Drew was stating the obvious. And he was. Any human who could avoid a demon, any demon, for such a long length of time was pretty extraordinary.

He might admire this Talia Maris, but he was getting pretty damn sick of coming up empty-handed, his mission not yet accomplished. The demon world was getting crazy, and he needed to end this task soon, get back to his normal duties. Problem was, his oldest brother, Zach, had his head up his ass because he'd finally found his mate, and his youngest brother, Hunter, was just plain losing his mind. As the only currently sane Winston brother, it was even more important for him to get back to trying to contain the Evils. Zach's mating time with Kat could have been disastrous had Drew and Kristoff not cleaned up the mess behind some of the incidents that had occurred. The Evils were getting bolder and bolder, now revealing their presence to humans without worrying about the repercussions. After a messy battle in a restaurant during Kat and Zach's mating period, it had taken Drew and Kristoff days to clean up the mess and wipe the minds of the humans who had witnessed the event. Not to mention deleting any lasting evidence. Sentinel duties were so much easier to carry out in the days before smart phones, videos, cameras, and other technology. And Drew suspected that it wouldn't be the last cover-up he and Kristoff would need to do. The existence of demons had to be kept from humans or the whole world would probably collapse. The battle between the Sentinels and Evils had been invisible to mankind for thousands of years, and needed to remain that way.

Drew eyed the cheeky note again, trying to figure out this mystery woman he'd been chasing for so long.

This woman knows she's being pursued. Somehow she realizes I'm after her.

He had no idea *how* she knew, or why she was under Sentinel protection, but he had no doubts about the veracity of the information contained in the notes he invariably found whenever he arrived somewhere he thought she'd be, only to find that he'd missed her...again. Unfortunately, he had a collection of such short letters, every one of them basically the same.

She always knew when he was close to her, and she bolted, leaving behind another note.

Pulling a chocolate truffle from his pocket, he removed the gold foil, popping it into his mouth with a thoughtful expression. Maybe it was time to change his strategy.

Drew turned his head, eyeing the lazy cat that was still watching him cautiously, a small grin beginning to form on his face, his expression turning wicked as a plan formed in his mind. Fine. If he couldn't get her to stay in one place, he'd have to give her a reason to talk to him. Looking at the overfed, well-groomed cat with a sparkly collar around its neck, Drew figured there might be something that she cared about enough to meet with him.

"I have some nice, juicy *tuna* at home," he told the cat cautiously, shuddering at the thought of getting anywhere near the feline.

The tabby, obviously familiar with *that* word, lifted its chin interestedly.

Drew felt just the tiniest bit guilty about kidnapping a pet the woman obviously loved. He manifested a cage around the cat, causing it to hiss and spit, a reaction he'd expected from the beginning, but he pushed his remorse aside.

It was time for he and Dr. Talia Maris to end this game, and he planned on being the winner. He *could* wait for her to return, but he doubted she would come back as long as he was here. Or, he could try to track her down once again in another place, but he knew those ideas were all fruitless pursuits. If she felt his presence, he could be waiting at her home in this rural area of northern Idaho forever. And she'd managed to avoid him everywhere else, too.

He wasn't going to get anywhere near her unless he took more drastic action, gave her a reason to *have* to talk to him, even if it did involve stealing a feline.

Drew stood, grasping the handle of the cat carrier, and cursed when the contrary animal clawed him through one of the openings, leaving a tear in his expensive leather jacket.

"Damn bloody nasty animal," Drew said, exasperated that he had to go to these lengths just to talk to a female who was, judging by some of her notes, probably as cantankerous as her cat. "I promised you tuna, for Christ's sake," he grumbled to the still surly animal, eyes narrowed at the cage and holding it away from his body in disgust.

Miraculously, the cat settled down, and was finally quiet.

Drew grimaced, realizing he had one thing in common with the angry animal.

They could both be motivated by food.

He disappeared, fervently hoping it wouldn't be long before the woman wanted to claim her cat.

Talia Maris pulled her SUV into her long, winding driveway with a sense of relief.

No demons.

She pushed her glasses awkwardly back onto the bridge of her nose, cursing the fact that she hadn't had the time or inclination to put in her contacts before she'd had to hastily leave her home. *Damn demons!* The lenses irritated her eyes, and she couldn't wear them all the time. Not that it really made a difference to her appearance. At five foot eleven, and taller than most men, her plain features and bland, shoulder-length brown hair were enough to make her unattractive, and contacts or not, she was an awkward, homely woman. Her dark green eyes were her only decent feature.

Talia sighed as she killed the engine, ready to finally be back home. At least the demons had left. She couldn't feel even the slightest demon presence. But she knew it was only a reprieve, and they'd be back soon enough. She'd been avoiding them for weeks now, and they always came back.

She grabbed the grocery bag on the seat and exited the vehicle, locking it behind her. Not that she really needed to worry. She lived in a small town, a rural area that rarely saw any crime. Although the townspeople probably considered her odd, which most people did, she'd always been safe since moving here after she'd finished graduate school. She'd been able to do her research on ancient history and write her texts and history books in peace to make a living. Until recently.

Why are the demons pursuing me now?

She hadn't been bothered by demons in years, not since Hunter had rescued her from making a deadly bargain with the Evils to try to save her mother's life. After the bargain with Hunter was done, she'd been under Sentinel protection, and hadn't seen or sensed a demon since, except an occasional guardian. And she'd liked it that way.

She didn't have any friends because the title of *Freak* had followed her wherever she went, and had for most of her life. And her mother, her only family, had died several years ago of cancer. So, Talia was an eccentric recluse who lived in her world of ancient history, her only real and loyal friend her orange tabby cat, Pumpkin.

Being alone is better than being hurt. Talia had learned that particular lesson a long time ago, and she was content with her life. She made a good living from writing textbooks and manuals, and she owned a home she could call her own.

I'm not lonely.

Okay, maybe there were moments when she wished she had someone to talk to other than her cat, but they quickly vanished when she thought about the teasing and taunting she'd endured while at school because she was a paranormal "sensitive," a woman who saw, felt, and sensed paranormal entities. Before she'd learned to control her abilities, she'd zone out, her green eyes glowing, as she had an encounter with ghosts and other supernatural beings. Any friends she'd started to make shunned her after the incidents, afraid of her abilities, seeing her as an oddity. Eventually, Talia had just given up trying, resigning herself to being a loner. It was preferable to being feared or ridiculed, and even though she now had control of her abilities for the most part, she still felt like the freak she'd been labeled earlier in life, even now at the age of nearly thirty.

Looking around the yard, she called for Pumpkin, surprised that her kitty wasn't waiting for her at the door. Talia had let her out before she'd left, and her feline was probably hungry. She frowned, looking at the note fluttering in the breeze taped on her door. She pulled it off with a yank, reading the lines with horror.

Dr. Maris,

I have your cat. If you decide you want to see it again, wait for me this time. I'm a Sentinel and I need to speak with you. I mean you no harm.

Drew

Talia unlocked the door, her body shaking with anger. How dare this monster make off with her Pumpkin! "Damn kitty-napper!" she sputtered as she walked through her small home to the kitchen, dropping the groceries on the counter, most of the bag containing Pumpkin's cat food.

She hastily scribbled a note on the back of the one left for her and slapped it angrily on the front door.

Frantic, Talia went back outside to look for her kitty, and then searched the inside of the house as well, unwilling to accept the fact that some despicable creature had actually taken her only friend away from her. She'd had Pumpkin since she'd been a kitten, finding her on her doorstep—weak, hungry, and shivering from the cold. The kitten hadn't cared that Talia was ugly and tall, eccentric and strange. Pumpkin had loved Talia because she'd taken care of the tiny ball of fur, feeding her and caring for her until she was strong again. From that time on, her cat had just given her unconditional love, something Talia hadn't had since her mother had become sick and died.

What if he hurts her? Talia felt ill at the thought that anyone could hurt Pumpkin.

She finally gave up searching, and flopped onto her couch, twisting a lock of her hair nervously as she thought about the note again. He said he was a Sentinel. So this demon was like Hunter, trying to protect humans. But that didn't mean he wouldn't harm her cat. Hunter had rescued her, but he was in no way what Talia would call kind or nice. Although Talia had never been afraid of him, or sensed true evil in him, he hadn't exactly been warm and fuzzy either. He'd been angry, disagreeable, and rude.

But he did save my life.

Whatever was pursuing her now was evil. Not all of the time, but often enough to send her hiding out until its essence disappeared. Thinking back, there may have been times when she actually didn't feel malicious intent, but she'd felt the presence of a demon, and that had been enough to make her flee.

The house was quiet, and Talia looked around her home, already feeling the gloom and emptiness without Pumpkin. The Sentinel had taken the one thing in the world that meant something to her, the one thing that brightened her solitary life. And she hated him for it.

"I want my cat back, you bastard," she screamed at the ceiling, as though the demon could hear her.

She didn't care if the Sentinel was a vile beast; she'd wait him out, and then she'd take his damn head off for taking an innocent animal to get what he wanted.

Talia looked over at her desk in the corner of her living room. Jumping up suddenly, she ran to her computer, searching through the stacks of neatly printed out papers next to it.

"Is everything here?" she muttered anxiously, sifting through the papers to check her research. Breathing a sigh of relief that the Sentinel probably hadn't come inside her home, Talia realized that it was all there, the stacks of research on demon history all in order.

Research. Learn. Discover.

"Damn it." Talia tried to fight the compulsion that drove her to find out more about the demons and their history, discover every detail she could about them. "Is there nothing that's under my control anymore?" she spat out, disgusted.

She'd started experiencing the compulsion to study demon history a few months ago, and she rarely got any relief. Her own ancient history projects had been put to the side, waiting until she got over these weird, uncontrollable urges to gather data on the demons. It wasn't that she wanted to do it; she *had* to do it. Personally, after Hunter had rescued her from the Evils, she'd never wanted to think about or see another demon again. But the overwhelming drive to find out about the demons wasn't her choice. Sometimes the obsession lasted for an hour or two, sometimes an entire day or days. The need to gather more information consumed her, beating at her mind and body until she had to go back to researching the demons or lose her mind.

In a daze, Talia brought her computer up and started to flip through her papers.

I need more information.

Really, what she wanted was to find her cat, but the urge to research was hitting her hard this time, and whatever *she* wanted was wiped out of her mind, her total focus centered on finding missing information on the demons.

She worked frenziedly, her fingers flying over computer keys, like a crazed woman who either had to find answers or face dire consequences.

It was two hours later when Talia finally got control of herself again, her delirium calming as she documented some of the information and conclusions she'd made on the demons during the last few hours.

Talia got out of the chair, still feeling dazed, and walked to the kitchen while shaking her head to try to clear her mind.

She looked at the clock, realizing that she hadn't missed an entire day. *Just a few hours this time.* Taking the cat food from the bag of groceries on the counter, she put it away, her hands still shaking.

What the hell is happening to me?

She didn't want to research demons, but it was like her mind and body were being controlled by something or someone else a hell of a lot more powerful than her. It was terrifying, unsettling, and the urges were getting closer and closer together.

Popping a low-calorie dinner in the microwave, Talia thought about the reasons this was happening, but she couldn't come up with anything other than it being something supernatural.

I thought I shut all that down years ago.

It wasn't that she didn't see paranormal entities anymore; she just didn't react to them. It had meant intense struggle and discipline to teach herself not to respond, but she'd finally been able to separate her emotions from seeing and feeling the otherworldly beings.

Taking her dinner into the living room, she sat on the couch, putting her food and a soda on the coffee table. Usually, Pumpkin would be right there, trying to discover if Talia had any food she wanted, and then turn up her kitty nose when she smelled nothing appetizing.

She wanted her cat back.

She wanted to not feel so damn alone.

She wanted to be normal and not feel compelled to research demons.

"I hate demons," she whispered fervently, a lone tear trickling down her cheek.

Her sorrow over losing her only loyal friend swamped her, along with the delayed reaction of her compulsive research frenzy.

For the first time in a very long time…Talia Maris buried her head in the pillow on the couch and wept, finally sobbing out all of her loneliness, unhappiness, and despair into the tattered pillow from her couch, wondering, now that she'd started, if she could ever stop.

Chapter Two

eow. Meow. Meow.

Drew scowled down at the pathetic creature at his feet, wondering what the hell the feline needed *now*. Its cry was plaintive and pleading, but he'd already opened his last can of tuna, and he didn't know what else to do.

Christ! He really did hate cats.

Several hours had passed, and he wondered if he could finally take the cursed feline back to the woman who owned it. Maybe the cat was homesick. Did that happen to cats?

Drew felt a pang of sympathy in his chest, and the thought of putting the animal back into the cage wasn't sitting right with him. He, of all creatures, knew what it was like to be caged and unable to escape. It was a Sentinel's greatest nightmare, and although he disliked this cat immensely, even he couldn't bring himself to be that cruel again.

Talk to the woman first and bargain with her. Leave the cat here. She can come and pick it up.

Meow!

He pulled another truffle from his pocket, stripped it, and put it in his mouth, ignoring the look of longing the cat was giving him. After chewing and swallowing, he looked down at the animal and told it adamantly , "Chocolate isn't good for you. Not something you want, believe me. You're better off sticking to fish." He'd read that somewhere, that chocolate was bad for cats and dogs. And the damn giant kitty had already devoured every can of tuna in his house. Certainly it couldn't possibly be hungry after its gluttonous orgy on several cans of fish.

Disgusted that he was actually talking to a cat, he transported slowly back to the woman's house, hoping to God that she was back and would take her behemoth pain-in-the-ass animal back to her home where it belonged.

He stopped outside her door, reading the note in front of his face with a grin.

Demon Bastard!

If you return, you'd better have my kidnapped cat, and she'd better be well and healthy or I'll cut off your balls and feed them to the wolves.

Yep. Obviously, the woman really loved her cat. He grimaced a little and put one hand to his groin over the comment about his balls. Obviously *that* was never going to happen, but he found it pretty gutsy that she'd even written those words to a demon.

Drew's hand stopped in mid-air as he reached for the note, his smile turning to a look of remorse as his attention was captured by the muffled, gut-wrenching sound of a woman sobbing. He listened for a minute, squirming on the doorstep, wondering if *he* was the cause of her distress. Really, could losing a wretched feline make a woman that unhappy?

The house went silent, and a moment later the door was swung open by a furious female, her face still damp from tears that she'd obviously tried to wipe away.

"Where's my Pumpkin?" she demanded, outraged.

Drew stepped into the wide open door, gaping at the woman in shocked surprise. "Pumpkin?" he croaked. "Please don't tell me you named your enormous spawn of Satan after a vegetable."

"A pumpkin is not a vegetable; it's a fruit. In fact, it's actually a berry. Pumpkins belong to the family Cucurbitaceae, which includes cucumbers, melons, squash, and gourds," Talia answered indignantly. "And I named her that because she's the same pretty orange color as a ripe pumpkin. Where is she?"

Okay, the cat was a female. Drew hadn't had any desire to find out. "Safe. In fact, she's just finished cleaning out my stock of tuna. How did you know I was here?"

He flinched as the female slammed the door behind him.

"I felt your slimy demon presence," she informed him with loathing in her voice.

"I'm a Sentinel," he replied indignantly.

"Same difference," she challenged. "A demon is a demon. You're obviously the type of beast who hurts an innocent animal to get what he wants."

"I didn't hurt your damn cat, woman," he answered, getting irritated. He was a Sentinel, and he wasn't evil. Maybe a little underhanded, but he hadn't exactly had nefarious intentions.

"You stole her from the only home she's ever known. I've had her since she was a kitten," she answered hotly.

Drew watched Talia as she strode across the room. She wasn't swaying her hips seductively or moving in any sensual way, but his eyes surveyed her regal walk, her tall, statuesque frame accentuating the sexiest, longest legs he'd ever seen. Her curvy hips were the type that a man wanted to grasp onto as he was slamming his cock inside her.

She turned and he met her fiery green eyes. Yeah, she was angry, but she chewed on her full bottom lip nervously, the whole package bringing to mind a woman of fire and ice, a fierce female who was also vulnerable. And he suddenly wanted nothing more than to protect her, take away the pain he could sense inside her.

Tapping her foot impatiently, she crossed her arms in front of her. "Well, are you giving me Pumpkin or not?"

Bloody hell! Drew felt a spark light in his soul, and he cringed at the pain it caused, almost like the eye's reaction to a bright light suddenly being turned on in a darkened room. It was jarring, and he was more than a little stunned.

He opened his mouth to speak, and then closed it again, realizing exactly what was happening. His eyes narrowed on Talia, mesmerized by her every feature. Even the glasses perched on her nose looked adorable.

His cock hardened like a rock, and the light in his soul grew even brighter.

Oh, hell no.

His mind tried to deny it, but he couldn't ignore the reaction happening in the rest of his body.

The woman he'd been tracking for over a month, the woman who avoided him like the plague, Dr. Talia Maris, was his *radiant*.

The Sentinel was staring at her, saying nothing, and Talia was looking right back at him, but his intense scrutiny was starting to unnerve her.

As she returned his stare, she admitted to herself that Drew was far from being a vile beast. He was more like a supercharged sexual fantasy. His slightly lilting Irish accent wasn't heavy, but it was there, making him even hotter. And he was plenty hot enough already. His eyes were dark and broody; his midnight-dark hair was neatly cut, but messy enough to conjure heated thoughts of disheveling it even more. And God, he was tall. Talia had spent her entire life being as tall as or taller than most men, but Drew towered over her in a way that made her feel almost dainty. He had a build to match his height, powerful shoulders filling out a black leather jacket to perfection, and a massive chest, every inch of him appearing to be solid muscle. Talia could see a pair of shiny black boots peeking out from under a pair of jeans that molded to him like a well-fitted glove.

"If you had stopped running away from me, I wouldn't have had to steal your cat just to have a conversation," Drew told her huskily.

"Why do you need to talk to me? I haven't seen a demon in years, not since Hunter rescued me and put me under Sentinel protection. I haven't even felt anything except the guardian Sentinels since then. Until recently. Now it's like every Evil in the western United States is after me." Talia sat down on the couch, feeling emotionally drained.

"How do you know it wasn't me? And how do you feel demons, anyway?" Drew questioned hoarsely. "Incidentally, Hunter just happens to be my brother."

Talia was a little startled that Drew and Hunter were related. Yeah, Hunter was attractive in an angry kind of way, but other than the dark coloring, they didn't look anything alike. "I'm sensitive to all things paranormal. I have been as long as I can remember. I'm a freak, a woman who can sense otherworldly beings. I can sense the Evils. I know if they're malevolent or not. The guardians feel peaceful. Other demons don't. When you arrived just now, I sensed your demon presence, that you weren't a guardian, but I could tell you weren't an Evil." Talia sighed and hugged the wet pillow she'd been crying on to her chest. "I guess I just started ditching any demon except the guardians in the last few months. I didn't stop to consider whether you were evil or not."

"You're being pursued by Evils?" Drew asked, his eyes narrowing dangerously.

"Yes. I don't know why. I'm under Sentinel protection. I nearly made a bargain with the Evils to try to save my mother's life. Hunter got to me just in time."

Drew sat on the other end of the couch, bringing them eye-to-eye. "Bastards," he muttered under his breath. Louder, he said, "You have to stop your research, Talia. That's why I was looking for you. It needs to be destroyed and I need your promise that you'll stop. What do you think would happen if the general public learned about our existence?"

She knew very well what would happen: hysteria, chaos, mayhem, and panic of epic proportions. It wasn't as if Talia didn't know that, but she wasn't doing this to *out* the demons to the world. "I can't stop," she answered desperately. "And you can't destroy my research. I'm not going to tell anyone. Please." Just the thought of Drew destroying her research was putting her into a panic.

Drew got up and sauntered over to her desk in the corner. "Is this it?"

Talia sprang off the couch, slamming into Drew in an effort to keep him from touching her work. "No, dammit. You can't do this." She started to hyperventilate, sweat starting to run down her face in tiny rivulets. She scooped up the tall pile of documents, holding her research to her chest protectively. "I'm not going to tell anyone. I'm not doing this for anyone else but myself."

"Calm down, woman," Drew said calmly. "It's just information."

"It's more than that to me. I hate demons. I never wanted to see one ever again after the incident with Hunter. But a few months ago, I started getting compulsions, painful episodes that made me research, made me document. I can't explain it to you, but it's something I have to do. I can't stop or I would. I have my own projects I need to get done." Her chest heaving, a death grip on her research, she stared at him pleadingly. "It's something I can't control, and if you destroy it or stop me, I think I might just lose my mind." Talia couldn't believe she was actually sharing this information with Drew, but she didn't see any other way to explain.

"Painful?" Drew asked, confused. "It actually hurts you?"

She nodded reluctantly. "Physically and emotionally. I zone out for a while, lose time. Sometimes I come out of it in an hour or two. Sometimes it takes a day. Or longer. I'm not doing this because I want to. I'm doing it because I can't *not* do it. I think it's something supernatural, but I don't know what."

"What does it feel like? What's driving you?" Drew asked, his brows drawing together in concern.

"I don't know," Talia answered dejectedly. "But it scares me. I used to be very normal, very boring. I worked on my ancient history research and wrote my text for work. But I wasn't obsessed; I wasn't crazy. Now I feel like I'm losing it."

"Put the papers down, Talia. I wouldn't do anything that would hurt you. Trust me." Drew's eyes turned dark and intense, but his voice remained reassuring and warm.

Her grip on the pile of data loosened, but she didn't put it down. "I don't trust anyone," she answered honestly.

"Except Pumpkin?" Drew teased, a small dimple appearing on his cheek as he grinned.

"I've found animals to be very reliable," she answered defensively. "People other than my deceased mother? Not so much."

Drew approached her slowly and pried the documents out of her hands, putting them back on the desk and leading her over to the couch. "Sit," he demanded.

Talia sat. She didn't know why, but for some unknown reason she really wanted to trust Drew. There was something about him that drew her to him, and it wasn't just the fact that he was a hot male with a sexy dimple. "I can't lose my research, Drew. I won't."

"Something tells me you won't need it," he replied roughly, crouching down in front of her.

"Of course I will," she answered, ready to jump up again to grab her papers, but Drew blocked her with his massive body.

"Listen to me," he insisted gruffly. "I don't know why this is happening to you, but we'll figure it out. I can't hurt you, Talia. It isn't possible. You're my *radiant.*"

In all of her research, Talia had never heard that term before. "Your what?" she queried, confused.

"My mate," Drew clarified. "Every Sentinel has a chosen mate, one woman who can lighten their soul. You're that woman for me."

Talia just gaped at Drew, unable to speak for a moment. She looked at the devilishly handsome Sentinel in complete and utter shock. "Me?" she squeaked. "Not possible."

"I'm afraid it is possible, and I'm telling you the truth. You *are* my mate," he repeated gravely, his dark, liquid eyes shining with sincerity. "It's not possible for me to do anything to harm you. My only instincts are to protect you."

Talia shook her head in disbelief. "You must be mistaken. How do you know?"

"Believe me, I'm not wrong," he answered huskily, reaching out to grasp her hand.

Talia felt the connection immediately, a strange force tugging her toward Drew. It was electric, exciting, and absolutely terrifying. "Taking Pumpkin away hurt me," she pointed out nervously.

"I'm sorry. I didn't know you were my mate until I saw you. I'll give her back. She's fine."

Talia tilted her head, assessing him. "Isn't she the sweetest cat in the world?"

"I wouldn't know," Drew replied glumly. "I hate cats."

Talia gasped. "How can you hate cats? Pumpkin has been the only real friend I've ever had."

"Cats aren't friends. They're animals. And cats hate me as much as I hate them. They sense my demon."

"Animals make better friends than people sometimes. If you feed them, love them, and take care of them, they love you no matter what." Talia wasn't quite certain that her first statement was absolutely true because she'd never had real human friends. She was too much of a freak.

"Stop doing that. You aren't a freak," Drew growled.

Talia knew she hadn't said that aloud. "Are you reading my mind?" Now *that* was unsettling.

"Your thoughts flow to me naturally. It's normal for a Sentinel to hear the thoughts of his mate," Drew informed her calmly.

"It isn't natural for me. Stop it." Honestly, it was damn uncomfortable. She didn't want Drew to know her every thought.

"I'm a demon. I can't help myself. Your mind is a very intriguing place to be." Drew grinned at her mischievously.

There was that damn dimple again, and he looked so incredibly... edible. "This can't be right."

"It was as much of a surprise to me as it was to you, believe me," Drew informed her, moving to sit on the couch beside her.

Somehow, Talia doubted that. She was overwhelmed and confused. She pulled her hand from Drew's and clutched the pillow to her chest instead. "Can I have my cat back?" she asked quietly.

"You can have any damn thing you want," Drew agreed readily. "But you'll have to come and get her."

"Why didn't you just bring her?" Talia asked curiously.

"She doesn't like the carrier I made," he admitted unhappily.

"She doesn't like any carrier. You could have just held her," Talia pointed out.

Drew scowled. "I told you I don't like cats, and that includes actually picking them up."

"Then maybe you should think twice before you steal one." Talia laughed. She couldn't help herself. Drew looked so forlorn, and it was incredibly amusing to her that the big, bad Sentinel demon wouldn't touch a sweet kitty like Pumpkin.

"She's a menace. She ate all my tuna," Drew grumbled, pulling a truffle from his pocket and popping it into his mouth.

"She opened the cans herself?" Talia asked innocently.

"She was crying," Drew said defensively.

Talia smiled, watching Drew try to explain why he'd been so concerned about a whining cat. "If you drive me to your house, I'll get her."

"I live in Seattle," Drew answered. "It could be a long drive. I teleported."

"Then just take me that way and bring me back," Talia suggested, not blinking an eye about his mode of travel. She'd never done it, but she knew that was how demons usually moved.

"I'm not bringing you back," Drew informed her casually. "You're being pursued by Evils, and you're not safe here. I have no idea why they're after you, but they obviously are. You'll stay with me. You're my mate, and that's something we have to work out."

"It doesn't mean we have to do anything about it. You could find someone else." Strangely, that thought didn't sit well with her at all, and she felt a sharp, proprietary instinct as she said the words, a jolt of negative reaction to her own words fluttering in her belly. She didn't want him to find anyone else.

"There is no one else, Talia. A Sentinel has one mate. Period. There isn't anyone else for me but you." He turned to her, his eyes turbulent and stormy. "It isn't a choice, and you have no idea how I feel right now."

"How do you feel?" Talia wasn't sure why she asked. She could see the truth on his face. Gone were all traces of his earlier humor, the carefree look replaced with the expression of a predator that had found its prey.

Pressing her back against the arm of the sofa, his body imprisoned her, enthralling her with the heat radiating in waves from his muscular form. "Like a demon," he answered hoarsely, his eyes dropping possessively to her mouth.

Her whole body caught fire as his hot, demanding mouth suddenly captured and consumed hers. Drew's embrace momentarily enthralled her, and she wrapped her arms around his neck, opening to him as though it were the natural thing for her to do. The connection grew stronger as Drew deepened the sensual assault, exploring her mouth with a ferocity that made her breathless, her body going liquid, and her core flooding with urgent heat. Never had she known desire like this, the need to connect with another person so desperately. She met his tongue as he pillaged her mouth, the fiery ache in her belly growing intense.

Suddenly, her body froze, her senses pounded by approaching Evils. She wrenched her mouth away from Drew's, panting.

"Evils. I can sense them," she said urgently, feeling a level of malevolence like she'd never sensed before approaching. "They're powerful."

"Fuck!" Drew didn't doubt her instinct for even a second. His body tensed immediately and he wrapped his arms around her tightly. "Hold on to me," he commanded.

She didn't have much time to react before she was plunged into darkness, clinging to Drew as the world grew dim and tilted wildly before fading to black.

Chapter Three

"**You** failed to tell me that the woman I was pursuing was actually my *radiant*." Drew was having a hell of a time holding his temper as he faced his Sentinel king, Kristoff Agares, who was lounging casually on a recliner in his massive living room. Drew had been torn between watching over Talia as she slept off her reaction to his rapid transport to his home, with Pumpkin curled up at her side, and finding Kristoff so he could tear his head off. Finally, he'd flashed away from Talia to Kristoff's home, his urgency for answers and information too tenacious to ignore. Talia was safe, and she was now his acknowledged mate. He'd sense it if she were in danger, now that they had met and were connected.

Drew couldn't sit, so he paced the floor in front of Kristoff, waiting for an answer.

"Did it ever occur to you that maybe I didn't know?" Kristoff swirled the Scotch in the glass he was holding, his brilliant blue eyes watching Drew pensively.

Bloody hell! Actually…no! Drew had no doubt in his mind that Kristoff had known exactly what he was doing when he'd sent Drew after Talia, had known that she was his *radiant*, and he was sick and tired of his king's cryptic answers. Instead of an answer, Kristoff had answered his question with a question. It was so damn irritating that

Drew was pushed not to go completely demon on his king, and it was unsettling. He respected Kristoff, owed him his very life, but he was damn tired of his sovereign's evasiveness. "You knew," Drew answered angrily, pulling a chocolate from his pocket and popping it into his mouth, even though his supply was getting low.

"You love being a Sentinel," Kristoff answered calmly. "A *radiant* is part of the deal. You always knew that."

Problem was, Drew *did* love being a Sentinel. While some other Sentinels had a love/hate relationship with their duties, Drew embraced them. He had a beautiful home outside of Seattle, and every toy a man—or demon—could ever desire. Best of all...he had an endless supply of food—any kind of food he wanted. He was a billionaire and would be for eternity. It was what he had wanted in return for becoming a Sentinel, and he'd gotten far more money than he'd ever dreamed he could have. He was one of the three Winston brothers, and he co-owned one of the wealthiest corporations in the world with Zach and Hunter. Though they weren't related by blood, the three Winstons were brothers in every other way, and closer than most siblings. "I don't need a *radiant*. I'm already happy."

"On the surface, perhaps, but no Sentinel is truly happy without a *radiant*." Kristoff's expression was thoughtful as he watched Drew pacing the room.

"I am," Drew answered adamantly, stopping for a moment to send Kristoff an irritated look. "Besides, I don't think Talia and I are well matched. She's actually *Dr.* Maris, and a sought-after authority on ancient history. Christ, she's fluent in four different languages, including Latin. What could the two of us possibly have in common?" Drew had been an Irish peasant, and he hadn't even been able to read before Kristoff had brought him into the Sentinel world. Yeah. Okay. He could read *now*. He liked to read. But he was no match for a woman as brilliant as Talia.

Kristoff shrugged. "She's your *radiant*. You wouldn't be matched if you didn't need each other, if you weren't destined to be together. And you do need her, Drew. Maybe you don't want to admit it right now, but she *is* your match."

Oh, Drew could easily admit that he wanted her, that he had definitely experienced the typical Sentinel reaction to a mate: a feeling of possessiveness and protectiveness so extreme that it was damn near uncontrollable. His soul longed to be joined with her light, and he wanted to fuck her until they were both so sated they couldn't move. Bloody hell! If this torturous need that he was feeling was what Zach had experienced with Kat, he wished he had been more sympathetic to his brother when he and Kat were suffering through the mating process. "I don't want this," Drew denied quietly, knowing his words were a lie even as they left his mouth. Maybe he hadn't ever wanted a *radiant* because he didn't have one. But now that he had Talia, he didn't really want to give her up. Maybe he'd never noticed the darkness of his soul because he'd never known anything different. Even as a human, he'd known very little except deprivation and loneliness. But the moment he'd recognized Talia as his *radiant*, the spark of light had ignited inside him, and he didn't want to let that go. She was extraordinary, and she was his. Maybe on the surface, they had nothing in common. But that didn't change the way he felt, the sense of rightness that had clicked into place from the moment he experienced the emotions and the spark of fire that lit his soul as he recognized the woman who was meant for him.

"Okay…then don't mate with her," Kristoff said, the corners of his mouth twitching as though he were trying not to smile. "Just do what you do best and protect her." Kristoff let out a masculine sigh. "You've always been the protector, Drew, the Winston who covers all the details. When the mess happened with Kat and Zach, you were there to do damage control before I was, to keep the Sentinels and Evils from being unveiled. You watch over Hunter, and you keep Zach from rushing into anything irrational. Talia's bold, probably braver than she should be when she's dealing with demons. Obviously, she's been confronted with paranormal beings her entire life. Her lack of fear is actually a weakness for her right now. She has no idea what the ancient Evils are actually capable of doing to her if they find her."

Tired of pacing, Drew flopped into a chair across from Kristoff. "She's being pursued by Evils," he admitted to Kristoff. "She's psychic, so she's escaped most confrontations with them, and that's why she was able to elude me for so damn long. But they want her. Why? She's under Sentinel protection. She was one of Hunter's rescues."

Kristoff hesitated for a moment before answering, "For the same reason they were after Kat. She's special, Drew."

Drew's head jerked up and he looked at Kristoff warily. "Why? What dormant power does she have? Are you saying she has a power like Kat does? Realm-walking?" Fuck! He didn't want Talia to be in danger because she possessed a greater power than most *radiants*. He wanted her safe, and if she was a special *radiant* like Kat, she was way too much of a target for the Evils, something they'd covet and do just about anything to possess.

"No. She has a different latent ability."

"What?" Drew demanded to know.

"That isn't something you need to know right now, and I'm not even certain I'm completely correct in my assumptions," Kristoff replied, his expression remorseful.

"Fuck! Are you serious?" Drew felt his demon clawing inside him. If his mate was in danger or possessed a power that could harm her, he had to know. "Talia's already tormented by some kind of compulsion to find out everything about demon history. It's eating her alive. And you're holding back information that might help her?"

"This information won't help her," Kristoff answered irritably. "Tell her everything she needs to know. She's your *radiant*. You can answer all of her questions. Knowledge is the only thing that will bring her relief. Her bloodline to a demigod is obviously stronger than Kat's, a connection that's making her feel compelled to seek out information. Her situation is different. Her drive to find out about the demons is probably coming from her ancestors. Once you enlighten her on demon history, the compulsions should stop." Kristoff released a masculine sigh. "You know that *radiants* with powerful latent abilities are an unknown. I can speculate, but I don't have anything concrete as of yet."

"It just started a few months ago," Drew answered, wondering why it had only recently started, if Kristoff's information was correct. If the connections to a demigod were stronger, why hadn't this started earlier? "About the same time the Evils started to pursue her."

"There had to be some kind of trigger," Kristoff informed him. "Something that woke the demigod connection. That's the reason why the Evils can sense her so strongly now. She needs protection, Drew. She needs you. Protect her," Kristoff demanded in the voice of an authoritative king that he rarely used with any of the Winston brothers, but there was also a plea threaded through the command.

Drew rose, looking at his king warily. "You know her, don't you? You know everything about her."

Kristoff looked away from Drew, his eyes trained on the flames in the fireplace. "I don't know everything. I just know she hasn't had the easiest life. I've never even met her. But I've watched over her enough to know that she's special. So in that regard…I guess I'm fairly familiar with her."

"And you knew what she was doing and why she was doing it. You sent me to her because you knew she was my *radiant*." Drew was furious with the lack of forthcoming information from Kristoff.

"That's not exactly correct." Kristoff still wasn't looking at Drew.

"Fuck! Why can't you just be straight with all of us? Me, Zach, Hunter…any one of us would die for you, but you don't trust any of us," Drew bellowed, his anger rising up along with his sense of betrayal. He felt like he'd been set up completely, going into a situation without any of the knowledge Kristoff was privy to, and could have shared with him.

Kristoff came to his feet so fast he was only a blur of motion as he stood. "I trust you. I trust Hunter and Zach, too. But there's only so much I can say, only so much I'm allowed to share, only so much I actually know before it's time for me to know. I'm bound by my honor, and my honor is all I have left. Give me that, and trust me when I say I tell you everything I can!" Kristoff's massive body was quaking, his nostrils flaring. "If you think I enjoy not being able to share everything I know or suspect…you're wrong. It haunts me. But the survival of the Sentinels, and of the human race for that matter, depends on me following the goddamn rules," Kristoff boomed in a tortured growl.

Drew took a step back as he watched his king fight for control. Never, in all of the years he'd been serving Kristoff, had he seen his king lose his temper like this. "I trust you. I'm sorry. I guess I never really understood." Drew's gut clenched as he watched Kristoff's expression mellow out, his persona returning to that of his usual calm self. Truth was, he *did* trust Kristoff, and he hadn't known that his king acted the way he did because he was honor bound as king to do so, that he *had* to be that way for the survival of the Sentinels. "Why didn't you tell us? We always thought you were just being an asshole."

"Sometimes I am an asshole," Kristoff agreed ruefully. "I tried as best I could to let you know what position I was in. I had hoped my actions over the years would gain the trust of all of you," Kristoff answered quietly, his tone low and grave.

The past hundred or so years rolled through Drew's mind. Kristoff had been there every time one of his Sentinels really needed him, protecting them just as they protected humans. The only thing that had ever bothered Drew was Kristoff's evasiveness, his isolation. But he was king, and Drew supposed Kristoff was as close to them as he could possibly could be as a leader who wasn't able to share information. There was a lot of difference between being unable and being unwilling. "You're right. You've been a good king. And I've never had reason not to trust you."

Kristoff slapped him on the shoulder, and Drew returned the action as a show of loyalty and respect.

"The day will come when it will be time for you to know everything. I'll be able to be your friend as well as your king," Kristoff said huskily, as though he were trying to hold back his emotions.

Drew looked him in the eye and replied, "I already consider you a friend, and I respect you as our leader. I always have." Drew hated the solemn look on the face of a king who had always been loyal to his Sentinels. "I just think you're a royal pain in the ass sometimes."

Kristoff moved toward the fireplace, stopping before the flames. He looked at Drew and cocked a brow at him. "And you think you, Hunter, and Zach are always a riot to work with?"

Drew grinned at Kristoff. "Of course."

Kristoff snorted loudly. "Hunter and his blatant disregard for any rules when it comes to killing Evils should have him on my shit list every day. Zach is far from the perfect Sentinel with his impulsive behavior. And you…you drive me completely insane with your stubbornness. Rarely does a day go by when I don't want to take the three of you and knock your heads together."

"Why don't you?" Drew asked curiously, knowing very well that he and his brothers pushed Kristoff's patience sometimes.

"Because you're all loyal. And that trumps some of the other nonsense." He gave Drew a warning look before he added, "Most of the time."

Drew could feel Talia starting to stir. "Talia's waking up. I have to go," he said anxiously.

"For a man who doesn't want a *radiant*, you sound awfully concerned," Kristoff answered wryly.

Drew tried to explain. "She's beautiful, intelligent, and gifted. I don't understand why she's supposed to be mine." He honestly didn't get it, but somewhere deep inside him, she was already his, whether he was worthy of her or not.

Mine! My radiant.

"She has her own insecurities, Drew."

He knew that. Drew could read Talia's thoughts and see her memories. Granted, he'd only had a brief glimpse, but what he had seen troubled him. She hadn't seen much happiness in her twenty-nine years on this earth, and he wanted desperately to change that.

Talia was nearly completely awake now, and Drew could sense her distress. "I'm outta here. She needs me."

Drew disappeared in the blink of an eye, leaving Kristoff alone in his massive living room. Staring at the spot from which Drew had just disappeared, Kristoff mumbled, "That she does, my friend. More than you know. Take care of her." Kristoff let out a masculine sigh and went to pour himself another drink.

Drew flashed into his bedroom only to find Talia out of his bed and not in the room. His heart skipped a beat, but he didn't completely panic. He knew she was close, probably still in the house. He could feel her.

Talia! He sent her a mental message as well as roaring it aloud. He reached out with his senses, waiting until he located her and flashed to her location.

She was in the living room, dashing from one corner to another, obviously looking for something.

"Talia? What are you doing?" She looked panicked and upset, so he tried to keep his voice calm, even though seeing her in any kind of distress made him half crazy.

She whirled around to face him, her desolation showing on her face. "I need a computer, Drew. And my notes. Please."

It only took an instant for Drew to sense her pain. Her as yet inexplicable desire for knowledge about the demons was tearing her up, and he couldn't bear to see her suffering this much worry and pain. "Stop, Talia!" he commanded, striding across the room and taking her gently by the shoulders. "I can tell you everything you want to know. I'm better than a computer and your notes." He scooped her up into his arms. Seating himself on his leather couch, he pulled her head against his chest and gently rocked her. "Calm down now. Tell me what you need to know and I'll help you." Her whole body was trembling, her brain darting from question to question. "Sort it all out, Talia. What do you need to know first?"

Talia squirmed on his lap, and then finally let her head slump against his chest with a relieved sigh. "I need to know if what I've documented so far is correct," she mumbled frantically against his chest. "Was it accurate? Is that how the creation really happened? Is everything believed to be mythology actually reality?"

"Yes. It was all correct," Drew answered. In fact, it was terrifyingly accurate. He was surprised she had been able to piece that much information together. Then again, Talia was brilliant, and her mind functioned in a way that humbled him.

"Are you human or demon when you become a Sentinel?" Talia shot out her next question as soon as Drew answered. "You obviously aren't one of the ancient Sentinels, so you must have been converted like Hunter."

"Both, I suppose," he said thoughtfully. "Although I'm demon, the Sentinels have evolved, living in the human world, developing human traits. Not so hard to believe considering most of us were human at one time and we still appear as we did when we were human. We become demon after we're recruited as a human and changed, but we've developed humanity, so we really have two parts—the man and the demon. Most of the time our humanity can control the demon, except in certain circumstances."

Talia continued to shoot out question after question, and Drew answered every one of them, trying to explain the role of every Sentinel, and the traits of the Evils. He breathed a sigh of relief as he felt her frenzy begin to dissipate and her pain disappearing after he answered what seemed like a million questions.

Finally, she asked hesitantly, "Tell me about *radiants.*"

He stroked her silky hair as he answered. "Sentinels have souls, but they're dark and always remain that way unless they find their *radiant.* And when they find their *radiant,* they have a very hard time controlling their demon side."

"Why?" she asked curiously, the panic attack gone, replaced by simple curiosity, which Drew knew Talia had in abundance. She was too intelligent not to be incredibly inquisitive.

"Mating behavior is completely elemental, totally demon and incredibly strong. The demon eventually takes control because it's driven by a basic instinct so dominant that it triumphs over our developed humanity."

"What about love? Is it just need, or do mates truly love each other?"

Drew hesitated, knowing he was going to have a hard time explaining her question. "*Radiant* matching is mystical, two souls that were meant to be together. I think it goes deeper than human love. It's magical. But I've never seen mates who weren't madly in love, too."

"How do you know I'm your *radiant?* Maybe it's all a mistake—"

"No mistake," Drew growled, shifting her body slightly to relieve the pressure on his throbbing cock. While Talia had needed him to relieve her pain and distress, he'd been able to control his demon. But he was rapidly losing the battle to keep his demon instincts in check. "You were meant to be mine. I felt it almost immediately when we met. A small light ignited in my soul, and it grows brighter every moment I'm with you."

"I find it hard to believe you really find me physically attractive. I'm not, you know." She pulled her head back, tilting it slightly as she looked at him candidly.

"To me, you're absolute perfection. I see you through the eyes of your mate, and you're the most irresistible woman on the planet and always will be to me," Drew told her honestly, unable to comprehend that she didn't see her own desirability. "I'll never want another woman. A Sentinel never feels physical desire for another female after he meets his *radiant*." Really, Drew wasn't certain he'd even felt real desire. Sure, he fucked. But he'd never felt this kind of need, a wanting that went way beyond screwing, although his desperation to join with her physically was becoming more and more excruciating. And his need to shield and protect her was overwhelming. Kristoff had been right. Talia's inquisitive nature and lack of fear terrified the hell out of him. It was dangerous for her, and somehow, his role as the one to safeguard her against anything that would bring her harm was his strongest instinct.

Talia frowned at him. "I'm a freak, Drew. I always have been. There isn't anything remotely attractive about me. I'm too tall, too plain, too awkward…which adds up to being physically undesirable." Her tone was matter-of-fact, as though she were just stating research data.

Drew's demon rose within him in a protective, possessive fury. He remembered a few of her memories that he had seen, all of them leaving Talia feeling as if she were unlovable. Unable to contain the way he felt about her for another second, he let her slide off his lap and onto her back on the couch. He was on her in an instant, his body holding hers prisoner beneath him. "Don't ever say that again. There's not a damn thing wrong with you. Not one single flaw. In fact, I have no idea how we were paired. I shouldn't have a woman like you. But the fact is…you are my *radiant* for a reason, and I think that reason is because you need me to protect you, because God knows I want to keep you safe more than I've ever wanted to be a guardian to anyone. And you don't seem to have any sense of self-preservation." Drew nearly groaned as she licked her plump, succulent lips nervously as she gazed at him in confusion. "Why are you constantly putting yourself down?" he asked her huskily, mesmerized by the emerald green of her eyes.

"Maybe because I'm used to it, because everyone else except my mother always did," Talia answered breathlessly. "People don't take care of me, Drew. People make fun of me." She turned her head away from him, hiding her expression. "The only person I ever trusted was my mom, but I don't have a lot of memories of her taking care of me. She was sick for a long time, and I took care of her. I went to college mostly on scholarships, living at home with her until she died. She loved me, but I mostly took care of her." Talia sighed softly before continuing, "After she died, I moved to Idaho. I mostly just wanted an isolated place where I could work and be alone. And that's what I did. Every day, I get up and research. I don't really know a soul in town. But I was okay with that. It was better than being ridiculed. I get up, I work, I go to bed. That's me. That's my life. It isn't that I don't know fear, but I guess the fact that if I was gone from the earth tomorrow, not a single person would even notice, and that makes dying insignificant to me. Who would care? Who would ever notice except my cat?"

Drew's heart splintered as he listened to her words, spoken in such a matter-of-fact tone that it made it even harder to bear. Talia wasn't feeling sorry for herself, or being dramatic. This was really how she felt, what she'd experienced in her short life. "I'd care, *mo stór*," Drew answered, slipping unconsciously into his native Gaelic terms of endearment. Talia's sense of aloneness just amplified his protectiveness, his need to make sure she was never vulnerable again. *"Beidh mé tú a chosaint,"* Drew said adamantly, vowing to protect her.

Talia looked back at him, her brow furrowing in concentration. "I can't translate Gaelic," she murmured, obviously annoyed that she couldn't.

"Ah…a language that you actually can't translate, Dr. Maris?" Drew smiled down at her, waves of fierce possessiveness pounding at him. "It simply means that I'll protect you. I think it's way past time that somebody did. And I doubt I could stop myself anyway. I want to be your champion, Talia, the man you look to when you need anything."

"I don't look to anyone," she admitted softly. "I never really have."

"You will," Drew replied stubbornly. Stroking her brow, he tried to erase the confusion from her face. "Can you honestly say that you don't feel the connection between us?"

Bloody hell. Say you do! Drew needed her to feel at least a small amount of the elemental desires he was experiencing.

"Your eyes are glowing," she answered, her voice slightly awed.

"A sign of intense desire for my mate. A demon reaction. Does it frighten you?"

She shook her head. "No," she whispered softly. "My eyes do that sometimes when I sense or see something otherworldly. But not like yours, not that beautiful, bright amber color. And I do feel the connection, Drew. I just don't completely understand it. "

She looked vulnerable and he knew she tasted sweeter than anything he'd ever tasted before. Her words pierced his soul and he claimed her mouth with a savage passion that he couldn't hold back. She'd said the words he wanted to hear…but he lost it anyway, both his human and demon sighing with relief as she wrapped her arms around him and responded to his rough embrace with an innocent desire that completely tipped him right over the edge of human sanity.

Chapter Four

Talia had only been intimate with one man in her entire life; a boy, really—an eighteen-year-old immature asshole in college—and having sex with her had been part of his fraternity initiation. *Have sex with an ugly virgin and bring us proof.* That had been the initiation challenge, and Talia, being young and still aching for acceptance at the time, had fallen right into the seduction. It had been an awkward coupling that her left her wondering why women even had sex. The humiliation that followed when she found out about the boy's motives and the scorn he showed her afterward completely killed her desire to have sex ever again.

Now, Talia realized that she'd never really known desire. As she let herself become lost in Drew, his tongue explored her mouth like he had to touch and possess every inch of it. His rough claiming left her moaning against his lips and desperate for more.

This is longing. This is what it feels like when a man truly wants a woman. And definitely how it should be when a woman wanted a man.

Drew pulled his mouth from hers, his chest heaving as he commanded, "Don't think about *him*. Never think about *him*. You're mine to take care of now, Talia."

The possessiveness in his low, desperate voice had Talia squirming beneath him, his hard cock pressing against her core so tightly that she had no doubt that he desired her. "I don't think about him anymore. Not usually," she answered breathlessly, staring at the ferocity of his expression, and the glowing amber eyes that, rather than frightening her, inflamed her even more because she knew she was the cause of the reaction. Drew really did want to be her protector, her lover. And feeling wanted in those ways was heady and delicious.

"He hurt you," Drew answered furiously.

"A long time ago. It doesn't matter," she answered, tightening her arms around his neck and squeezing her legs around his hips. Truly, her past sexual humiliation really didn't matter. Drew, and her agonizing craving for him, wiped every other rational thought from her brain.

His vow to protect her had shattered some of the protective ice around her heart, breaking through to the woman who really had been lonely for so very long.

"I'll do nothing except pleasure you until that bad experience is completely gone from your mind," he told her huskily, arrogantly, but with a touch of vulnerability as well.

Oh hell, it was already gone. At that moment, Talia couldn't care less about some silly boy who had tried to take away her dignity along with her virginity when she was barely an adult. Right now, all she cared about was being possessed by this big, fierce, angry man/demon who was holding her body captive with his, and who wanted her more than anyone ever had. "I've forgotten about him already," she murmured softly, stroking the thick, coarse hair at Drew's nape. The corded muscles in his neck were tight and tense, just like his every other muscle she could feel. White-hot desire was smoldering from his body, and it was being absorbed by hers, the heat nearly incinerating her alive. "Please, Drew," she pleaded. Her gaze locked with his as her entire being pulsated with yearning for his touch, his possession.

"Christ! Do you two mind doing this later? I'm about to go blind here," another male voice grumbled irritably.

The sound of someone else in the room was enough to pull Talia from her haze of lust, her head jerking to the side to see an angry Hunter standing across the room. He was bruised, his face full of lacerations in various states of healing, and his expression looked completely disgusted.

He hadn't changed a bit. Hunter looked exactly like he had the last time she'd seen him.

Talia looked back and forth from Drew to Hunter, Drew's eyes never leaving her. "Drew…let me up. Hunter's here," she told him desperately, pushing against his chest frantically.

"Leave," Drew snarled, his eyes glowing even brighter as he looked briefly at Hunter and then back at Talia. "My mate."

"Oh, shit." Hunter rolled his eyes. "Not again." He flopped into a chair, not looking at all ready to leave. "Get off her, Irish." His eyes narrowed as they focused on Talia. "Hey, I know you."

Talia pushed harder on Drew's chest, trying to move what seemed like an unyielding mountain on top of her, embarrassed by Hunter's eagle-eyed stare. "Yes. We've met. You rescued me when I stupidly almost made the mistake of agreeing to an Evil bargain to save my mother."

Talia finally gave up trying to get Drew to move and rolled out from under him, landing on her ass in an awkward heap on the carpet. Drew's arm shot out and pulled her up beside him, his steely arm wrapped around her waist. Sitting up, he pulled her beside him and drilled Hunter with a furious glare.

"Leave," Drew demanded again, his voice dripping with hostility.

"Take it easy. I'm not taking her from you. I acknowledge that she's yours," Hunter answered, looking exasperated.

Talia felt Drew's body slowly relax beside her as she asked shakily, "You remember me?" At that moment, Pumpkin came into the living room and leaped up onto Talia's lap, as if sensing that her presence was needed to defuse the moment. Talia petted her cat with a shaky hand. "I can't believe you're Drew's brother."

"I remember all of my rescues," Hunter rumbled. "And he *is* my brother."

"And mine," another voice echoed as Zachary Winston appeared in the room, only feet away from the couch. He approached slowly and held his hand out to Talia. "Zach Winston," he introduced himself. "The third Winston brother."

Zach's smile was calm and polite, a welcome change from Hunter's brittle, mocking smirk. Talia shook his hand briefly, and Zach moved back to sit in a recliner next to Hunter.

Talia gaped at the two brothers and then turned back to Drew. "Winston? Like in the billionaire Winston brothers?" She might be isolated, but she'd have to be living under a rock not to have heard of the Winston brothers. They were assumed to be excessively reclusive, and were never photographed. Now she knew why. Obviously they didn't get around like normal people, and if they didn't want photos of themselves out there, that problem could be easily resolved.

"Yes." Drew acknowledged the brothers' identity. "What the hell are you doing here?" Drew asked both his brothers impatiently.

Zach answered patiently, "We had plans, Drew. We all agreed to meet here at seven o'clock so we could try out that new Mexican restaurant. You know…food…your favorite thing in the world." He shot Drew a questioning look before adding, "Until today, I guess."

"I forgot," Drew answered in an agitated voice.

"I get it. I just left Kristoff's—he filled me in," Zach informed Drew.

"Talia's being pursued by powerful Evils, probably ancients," Drew told his brothers, running a hand through his hair, frustrated.

"I'll fucking kill them all," Hunter growled. "She was my rescue."

Zach sent a swift warning glance at Hunter before continuing, "For some reason, they're after her. She's special, just like Kat." Zach's features softened as he mentioned his mate's name. "They aren't going to stop looking just because you relocated."

Drew groaned. "I know. I need to find a place where she's going to be safe."

"Being with you is the safest place she can be right now," Zach answered sympathetically. "If Talia can really sense the Evils like Kristoff said she can, you can move locations if they find you here. She's special. That's why they want her. And I doubt they'll give up easily."

Talia glanced from one brother to the other before asking, "Special how? I don't understand." How was she any different from any other *radiant*?

Zach quickly explained how his mate, Kat, was a realm-walker, and he went through the series of events that had occurred after he and Kat had met. Talia listened with fascination, stunned. "So her powers were released when you bound yourself together? Do I have the same dormant power?"

"No." Drew answered this time. "Your power is probably just as strong, but different. Kristoff, our king, says they're not the same as Kat's, but we won't know exactly what they are until the power is released."

"I'm already psychic. I see paranormal beings when other people don't. Is that all part of this dormant power?" She'd always been different. Maybe now she actually knew why.

"Honestly, I don't know. But Kat isn't psychic and never was," Drew responded, his arm tightening around Talia's waist in silent support. "And you aren't different. You're special."

Talia grimaced, but she secretly adored Drew's emphatic declaration.

"Can we discuss this while we're eating? I'm hungry, Irish," Hunter grumbled.

"I have to agree," Zach agreed sheepishly. "Kat has a class tonight and I don't want to eat my own cooking." He briefly explained to Talia that his wife was going back to school to get her degree, leaving him on his own for the evening.

Drew looked at Talia. "Are you hungry?"

Almost as if on cue, Talia's stomach rumbled. She'd been under compulsion earlier in the day and hadn't eaten. "Actually…yeah."

"We'll go," Drew informed his brothers as he stood, pulling Talia up beside him. Pumpkin slid off Talia's lap and landed on the couch, giving Drew an indignant look. "But I'll drive. Talia already had to recover from rapid transport once today."

Hunter and Zach stood up, neither one of them looking happy that they'd have to wait at the restaurant for Drew.

"Go ahead. I can grab something here," Talia told Drew, not wanting anyone to have to wait for her.

"Over my dead body," Drew rasped. "You stay with me. They can wait, right?" He shot his two brothers an answer-yes-or-I'll-kill-you look.

Zach nodded, any sign of impatience gone. "Of course. It isn't that far away."

"I'm ordering," Hunter warned Drew. "And I'm eating all the chips while I'm waiting."

Talia laughed, amused by Hunter's refusal to be polite. He'd never exactly been warm and fuzzy, and that hadn't changed a bit. The difference was...now she could see the spark of pain in his eyes, something she'd never noticed before. "We'll order more," she shot back at him.

"I'll eat those too," Hunter replied wickedly, disappearing in front of her eyes before she could blink.

"Bastard," Drew commented testily.

"I'll save you some," Zach comforted Drew, grinning at Talia. "Ordinarily, nothing gets between Drew and his food." Zach winked at Talia and disappeared.

"I'm sorry," Talia told Drew remorsefully. "We could try to transport. Can't you go slower?"

She shivered as he lowered his head, his lips grazing the side of her neck, pulling her back against him as his mouth wandered to her ear. He was so damn...tall. Talia had felt like a giant beside almost all women and some men most of her life, but Drew towered behind her... big, solid, and so very warm. She relaxed into his embrace, tipping her head to give him access as he nuzzled her ear, his warm breath caressing the sensitive flesh.

"*Mo stór*...with you...I doubt the word 'slow' is even part of my vocabulary," he answered gruffly, sounding pained.

Although Talia couldn't translate Irish Gaelic, she did understand the Irish endearment that was akin to him calling her his darling, and she let the low, sexy voice wash over her heart like a balm. She bent and scooped up a handful of candy from a dish on the coffee table. "Maybe these will tide you over until we get to the restaurant," she suggested, holding the handful of chocolate out to him.

He turned her around and looked down at her, his grin mischievous and playful. He grabbed the dish and emptied the whole thing into his pocket. "Keep those for yourself. I'm restocked."

Giving Drew an exasperated look, she dropped the candy back into the dish. "We're already going to eat Mexican food. I won't get thin eating like that." Her hips were already a little too curvy, and she could stand to lose a few pounds. Her research and writing made for a pretty sedentary lifestyle.

Drew's expression grew suddenly stormy. "Don't say that. Don't ever get thin," he answered desperately, his eyes turning wild. He pulled a gold foil-wrapped treat from his pocket and tore off the wrapper. "Open," he demanded, holding the decadent chocolate to her mouth.

He looked so anxious that Talia obeyed, eying his wild-eyed panic mixed with concern. The burst of sweetness that exploded inside her mouth was so divine that she had to swallow back a moan. "That's good." The man definitely knew his chocolate. It was one of the most decadent things she'd ever tasted.

She watched as he frantically opened another and held it up to her. She opened her mouth and accepted it, but shook her head as he held up yet another. Swallowing hard, she told him, "That's enough."

"Thin isn't good, Talia. It's bad. Eat," he demanded, his expression stubborn.

"Drew, I don't think I'm in any danger of getting too skinny." She searched his face, trying to figure out what was motivating his behavior. Obviously, it was some sort of protectiveness, something Drew seemed to have in abundance. "I have plenty of extra meat on my bones." *More than enough.*

"Never enough," Drew answered harshly. "I'll always have plenty of food. You'll never go hungry."

"You went hungry at one time, didn't you?" Her mind calculating quickly, thinking about his year of birth, she asked gently, "Were you in Ireland during the potato famine?"

He held the treat patiently at her mouth, waiting for her to take it, and finally, she did. Not that she wanted or needed it, but she couldn't bear the look on his face. His expression was haunted as he watched her chew and swallow before he finally answered. "Yes. My parents died when I was young and I tried to take over their small plot of land to farm. We were poor. Always poor. But after my parents died, I was at least able to survive on some of the potatoes. When the potatoes went bad, there was no food. I ate whatever I could find, even the bark from trees, to try to survive. I was nearly dead when Kristoff found me."

Talia closed her eyes in horror, unable to keep herself from picturing an emaciated Drew, near death from starvation. The Great Famine during the mid-nineteenth century had killed more than a million people in Ireland due to a potato blight. Knowing Drew had suffered through most of it was almost unbearable. It had been a hellish, dreadful time in Irish history, and for a poor farmer like Drew, she could only imagine the suffering he'd witnessed and experienced. "Kristoff saved you," she murmured, wrapping her arms around Drew's waist and laying her head on his shoulder.

"It was a near miss," Drew admitted huskily. "I was delirious, sick with one of the diseases running rampant through Ireland. I thought he was a delusion at first." He released a masculine sigh. "But yeah…he saved my life. I never could figure out why. I was dying. I wasn't straddling the line between good and evil. I had already stolen, begged, and done evil things just to try to stay alive. I'd given up."

"Because you were worth saving," Talia answered emphatically, her heart still breaking at the thought of Drew being so hungry for so many years. No wonder he ate all the time. Had she gone through the kind of deprivation that she knew had happened during the Great Famine, she'd be doing the same.

"So sure of that, are you?" Drew questioned softly, his tone slightly amused, his Irish brogue more prominent.

"Yes," she answered honestly, pulling back to look up at him, amazed that she actually had to tilt her head back to see any man, given her height. "It must have taken incredible strength to have lived as long as you did. When did he rescue you?"

"Eighteen forty-eight. I hadn't even hit my thirtieth birthday yet, and I was already dead," Drew replied, his massive body shuddering slightly, obviously still reliving the memories of his past.

"How long had you been starving?" Talia couldn't keep herself from asking, even though she didn't want to think about it. Drew obviously needed to put some of those memories to rest. "And you weren't really dead."

"Very nearly. I was hungry for years, but by the time Kristoff arrived, you could see every bone in my body. I didn't have anything left, and I knew whatever disease had taken hold of me was going to kill me."

He'd been a skeleton ready to die. Talia felt a tear trickle down her cheek. Although she studied ancient history, she was familiar with the horrors of the Great Famine. "Were you afraid?"

Talia could feel Drew shaking his head. "No. By then I just wanted to die," he admitted. "I prayed for death. I know what it's like to not care if you live or die, to know that your presence on earth won't be missed by one single person."

More tears poured down her face and Drew gently wiped them away as they fell. "What would have happened to you if Kristoff hadn't found you in time?" she said, her voice choked with emotion.

"Don't agitate yourself, mo stór. It was long ago. I survived."

Talia lifted her hand to his whiskered jaw. "I suddenly want to feed you. Desperately. Can you transport us slowly to the restaurant?"

Drew frowned at her. "I can, but I won't. I won't risk it. Besides, I'm not all that certain that my hunger is for food anymore. I'm more concerned about getting you food." He took her hand as he wiped away the last tear on her face. "I'm beginning to think it never really was food that I actually wanted," he finished huskily, his eyes liquid and dark.

Talia knew Drew ate just because he could, and because he'd never gotten over his period of starvation. Perhaps he really didn't need food at the moment, but after hearing his story, she wanted to see him eat. Her stomach growled, and she thought it was probably more in empathy for Drew than her own need. Her connection to him grew stronger every moment that she was near him. "Well, then feed me," she told him with a chuckle.

"We'll go now," Drew replied tensely. "I know you're hungry."

Hungry for you.

The turbulent look in his eyes told Talia he heard her thoughts. "And stop reading my mind," she scolded, slapping him on the arm. "Feed me."

He grinned wickedly. "I'm a demon, *mo mhuirnín*. Some things are not controllable." He took her hand in hers. "Ready?"

"Yes." Talia knew she was getting way too accustomed to Drew calling her his treasure, his darling, or his dear in Gaelic, and it was much too sexy said in his flowing baritone, rolling off his tongue so naturally. But it made her feel…cherished. Much like Drew could read her thoughts, she could sense his emotions, and the words were natural for him, an expression in his native tongue of his feelings for her.

He nodded once and took them to the restaurant, even driving more cautiously because she was in the vehicle. Maybe she shouldn't become accustomed to it, but for the first time in her life, a man actually held her as something dear to him, and it felt so damn good.

Chapter Five

"What's the mating ceremony like?" Talia asked the voluptuous, redheaded woman sitting across the kitchen table from her. Zach and Kat had come for a visit to Drew's home, and the two males were currently taking care of Sentinel business, leaving the women together at Drew's.

Talia could feel what seemed like a battalion of guardian Sentinels around them, no doubt put in place by Drew. When he'd promised to protect her, he hadn't been saying it lightly. When he was here, he rarely let her out of his sight. And when he was gone, she was surrounded by protection. It didn't matter that he could flash back to her in an instant whenever she called him. Despite this, it still took him a good five minutes to give her instructions about what to do should anything happen, and he made her promise that the first thing she would do was to call out to him.

He still claimed to hate cats, but Talia had caught him talking to Pumpkin before he left, stroking her fur and telling her to watch out for her owner. Like Pumpkin was a kitty version of a Doberman? Still, it had been such a touching scene between the self-professed feline-hater and her kitty that Talia had wanted to cry.

Talia had liked Kat immediately, sensing a kindred spirit almost from the moment they had met a few hours ago. Normally shy and quiet due to her isolation, Talia surprisingly found that she could talk easily and freely with Zach's wife. Kat had filled Talia in on the demon world from a *radiant's* perspective, which turned out to be quite different from the history she'd been gaining from Drew over the last week. Not that everything Drew had told her wasn't true, but it was different from a *radiant* point of view.

Kat took a sip of her coffee and flushed slightly. "I'm not sure I can explain it. Not because I don't want to, but because I can't think of anything comparable." After frowning in concentration for a moment, she added, "You know how you feel compelled to join with Drew, and that urgency just keeps getting worse?" Kat asked with a questioning look.

Oh, yeah. Talia knew. She'd been suffering through the effects of the mating instinct for the last week, finding it harder to resist with each passing day. But resist she did. She wanted to really know Drew, not be compelled by an ancient rule some god or goddess had decreed. Incredibly, Drew seemed to understand what she wanted, even though she knew it hadn't been easy for him. "Yes," she answered Kat's query softly.

"Well...it's sort of a culmination of all of the desire, need, and the emotions that go with it rolled into one...um...encounter, whipped around, and finally settling into place." Placing her mug back on the table, she shot Talia a mischievous glance. "It's like the most incredible orgasm imaginable, combined with intense relief. Once a Sentinel and a *radiant* merge, she gains a tiny piece of his soul, and he gets a sliver of hers, enough to flood his soul with light. It's like you're finally whole again after missing a part of yourself for a very long time." She smiled. "Admittedly, it was much longer for Zach than it was for me, but I don't think you really notice how much you were missing that part of yourself until you meet your mate." Kat reached up and slid down the neck of her long-sleeved shirt. "We both carry the mating mark."

Talia squinted at it before rising and walking around the table, examining the mark Kat was exposing. "May I look, touch it?"

"Be my guest," Kat agreed amiably, yanking the V-neck shirt lower.

Talia stroked one finger over the mark. It was hot, radiating a warmth that was supernatural. But she was more interested in the tiny markings. "Twin souls?" she wondered aloud. The depictions were identical, resembling two minuscule illuminated specks that united as one to make a perfect flame.

"What does it mean?" Kat asked curiously.

"Plato once wrote about twin souls in Greek mythology," Talia muttered thoughtfully. "He explained that humans were once both male and female, and that they had four legs, four arms, and two heads. When humans became too arrogant, Zeus split them in half so one part would yearn for the other eternally because their soul was separated and torn in half."

"Do you think it's true?" Kat asked as she pulled her shirt back up to her shoulder.

Talia took her seat again. "I study ancient history with scientific facts. I never believed in mythology at all until I met the demons. Now I'm forced to consider that everything I thought was truth really isn't. There's no proof that mythological creatures existed, but most people don't see ghosts and otherworldly visions," she grumbled unhappily. "But I suppose the *radiants* and Sentinels could have the same basic concept of twin souls, although I have no idea if the myth is actually true. The obvious conclusion I've made is that the ancient history I study is real…true scientific data, but only in one dimension."

"One realm," Kat added excitedly.

Talia gave Kat a weak smile. "Yes. Paranormal beings exist in another dimension. But somehow, the Sentinels exist in the same realm as we do, but the Evils don't, although they can visit this realm. And some entities occasionally pass through the barrier into the human realm for a variety of reasons."

Kat nodded. "Like me. I can walk realms, go to those other dimensions. Kristoff is working with me to control that power. Right now it's kind of a crapshoot where I'll end up if I try to leave the human realm, but I'm getting better."

Talia had recently met Kristoff, who she personally thought resembled both a god and man. He was physically beautiful, almost too perfect, and he emanated a power that was frightening. "I have a special power, too," she admitted to Kat. "But it's an unknown until it's released if I mate with Drew."

"Just be careful when you do. I know Zach told you what happened to me. You said 'if,'" Kat replied curiously. "Don't you want to be with Drew?"

Yes. Yes. Yes.

If the theory of *radiants* and Sentinels being similar to twin souls was correct, and if one soul really did complete the other, Drew was her match. Oh hell, she knew Drew was her partner soul. There was no other way to explain her yearning to be with him. She wasn't experiencing infatuation or a schoolgirl crush. The way she felt when she was around Drew was more like a super-powered magnet trying to suck her toward him, refusing to let go. "I've spent most of my adult life trying to avoid men. I'm a freak, Kat."

"You're not a freak!" Kat exclaimed furiously.

"I see the paranormal. My eyes glow when I spot one in the human realm. I'm taller than a lot of men, and I'm so ugly that the only sexual experience I've had in my life was a fraternity prank when I was in college to see who could sleep with an ugly virgin for initiation." She shot Kat a dubious look. "Freak," she repeated.

"You're statuesque and you have beautiful eyes," Kat defended angrily. "Maybe you're different, unique, but that doesn't make you a freak. And Drew thinks you're the most beautiful thing on earth. Do you really think I'm such a catch?" Kat gestured at her own body and face. "Until I met Zach, I didn't believe I was attractive. I've always been overweight, and my red hair has constantly been the bane of my life. But Zach still looks at me like I'm the most desirable woman he's ever seen. Give Drew some time. He'll eventually convince you because he'll never stop looking at you the way he does now." Kat stopped and took a deep breath. "Your IQ is off the charts. I'd love to be that smart. It's likely that the people in your life were just jealous. Do you have family?"

Talia felt a twinge of pain in her chest, a reminder of a time when she had a mother who loved her. "I never knew my father. I was the result of my mom's first and only one-nighter. But I lost my mother four years ago. Luckily, I was left enough money to survive, and had enough scholarships to finish school."

"Siblings?" Kat queried.

Talia lowered her head, remembering how alone she'd been almost her entire adult life except for her mother. When her only parent had died of cancer, she'd been completely alone. "No. I don't have anybody."

"You have all of us, now, Talia. The Sentinels will be your family," Kat said softly. "I've only been married to Zach for a little over a month, but I love Kristoff, Drew, and Hunter like brothers."

Somehow Talia couldn't see Hunter as a brotherly type of guy, and she told Kat her thoughts.

"Hunter's troubled," Kat admitted reluctantly. "But he lost his whole family to the Evils. He can't ever seem to get enough revenge to dissolve his anger. He cuts through the Evils like a madman, but he's kind to me. I think there's more to Hunter than anyone knows."

Talia had sensed that, and she'd never been afraid of Hunter, no matter how mad, bad, and angry he seemed. His vibes were volatile, but not evil.

"I think I'd really like to have family," Talia answered Kat honestly as she looked up at her. The other woman's eyes glowed with nothing but kindness, and Talia sensed that she'd found a friendship like she'd never known. She'd never been good with people, but Kat was somehow different. It was like the two women understood each other perfectly. "And I do want to be with Drew. But we barely know each other." *But then, why does it seem like we've known each other forever, yearned for each other for a lifetime and beyond?*

Kat leaned back in her chair and crossed her arms. "Patience isn't exactly a Sentinel virtue, but get to know him. Drew has always been the reasonable Winston, the one who watches over everyone else, takes care of everyone else. He asks for very little in return. Except food. He deserves so much more, someone of his own. No one will ever care about you more."

Talia wanted to get to know him in every way, including physically, but she answered aloud, "He's trying to be patient."

"Well, for a Sentinel in the mating process, it's pretty hard," Kat mused, smiling mischievously as she realized what she'd just said.

"It's always hard," Talia said with a laugh.

"Get used to it. It doesn't change after you're mated," Kat snickered. "Do you mind?"

"Nope," Kat replied smugly. "Not a bit. I think I'd be disappointed now if Zach wasn't so intense, although it took some getting used to."

Talia wasn't at all sure she'd have a difficult time getting used to being the object of Drew's unrelenting desire. In fact, she was pretty sure she'd relish it once she got past her initial reservations and apprehensions. Right now, it was overwhelming, but she was fairly certain that she was living every woman's fantasy with Drew.

"I think I could learn to live with that problem," she answered Kat with a playful wink.

"It's one of the perks of being a Sentinel's *radiant*," Kat corrected.

Talia reached out her arm and snatched a cookie to go with her coffee— one of Drew's favorite treats. *One of many!* She chewed, letting the taste of chocolate and pecans explode inside her mouth. She swallowed before remarking hesitantly, "I just don't want to disappoint him."

"Not possible," Kat said confidently.

Raising her coffee to her mouth, Talia hoped that Kat was right.

Drew watched as the penalty Sentinels prepared Hunter for another punishment, this time for decapitating two Evils without provocation. "Fuck! He can't take any more of this. He damned went through it yesterday," Drew said angrily to Zach, who standing at his side. "Why can't he just stop?"

Drew and Zach usually didn't watch the torture that their brother went through time after time for wasting Evils by the dozen. This time...they did. Hunter endured the penalties without complaint, but both brothers were concerned now, anxious that his sanity was starting to slip. Hunter broke the rules too often now, too close together, and it was taking its toll on him. He was already beaten and broken from yesterday's infractions. Two days in a row was going to be too much. One of them would have to step in, trying to safeguard Hunter's barely sound mind.

"Can't you stop them?" Drew asked furiously, jerking his head at Kristoff, who was standing on his other side.

"I'd take his place if I could. But I'm not allowed to interfere. Not in the human realm," Kristoff said regretfully. "But you're correct. I'm not sure he can take much more."

"I'll take his place," Zach answered, starting to step forward and toward the area where Hunter was about to take a beating.

"No!" There was no way Drew was letting Zach step in. Kat would kill him. He grasped Zach's upper arm to stop him. "You have a mate to think about."

"So do you," Zach said solemnly. "Let me go, Drew. You don't always have to be the one to step up to the plate all the time."

"You're not going," Drew replied adamantly, looking at Kristoff. "Permission to take Hunter's punishment?" he asked his king.

Kristoff's nod was nearly imperceptible. "Granted," he replied formally, his voice strong, but resonating with regret.

Zach yanked his arm away from Drew. "Goddammit, Drew. You'll be locked up all night."

"Take care of Talia. Swear it!" he demanded of both his king and his brother, looking from one to the other.

"Done," Kristoff and Zach answered in unison.

"Stubborn bastard," Zach rasped, watching as Drew strode forward to relieve Hunter of his punishment. It was the right of a Sentinel to take the disciplinary action for another with permission from their king.

Drew didn't hesitate. He came to a halt in front of the penalty Sentinel, blocking him from getting to Hunter. "I've been granted permission to take Hunter's place. Let him go."

The Sentinel who was to carry out Hunter's sentence lifted his head and spotted his king standing across the open courtyard. Kristoff nodded and Hunter was released. It took him only a moment to get Hunter completely free.

"No. Get on with it," Hunter told the penalty Sentinel. "I refuse to let him step in." Hunter's voice was hoarse and defiant.

The penalty Sentinel shrugged. "You can't refuse. It's an order from our king."

It took several guards to take Hunter away, dragging him to Kristoff's side. Drew breathed a sigh of relief as he saw all of them flash away—Hunter definitely not leaving by choice as Kristoff wrapped a powerful arm around his neck and transported out of sight.

They'll take care of Talia.

Truth was, he didn't want anyone watching over Talia except him. It wasn't that he didn't trust Zach and Kristoff, but he needed and wanted to see her, to protect her. His mating instincts were screaming painfully at him to go to her, but he was bound by his word, and he *would* serve Hunter's sentence. His brother was just a short step away from losing his mind, and he was afraid that any further punishment would send Hunter tumbling over the edge.

"You ready?" the Sentinel standing next to Drew asked stoically.

Drew didn't bother doing things the human way. He wanted to get this over with as quickly as possible. He made his clothing disappear magically, leaving himself completely nude.

A prolonged beating was first, followed by incarceration in the isolation cell. Sentinel demons couldn't bear to be confined, and it was the worst sort of torment for them to have to live through being in the tiny prison with no escape. The cubicle was mystical, and Drew knew he'd be powerless the entire night. Not that he'd try to leave. Hunter's fuck-up had to be punished, and the slate wouldn't be clean until his time was served.

Drew gritted his teeth as he was bound to a brick wall, the captivity enough to irritate him.

The first crack of the whip hurt. The second was a bit more excruciating. He tried to think about Talia, how his whole life had changed since she'd entered it. Her beauty took his breath away, and everything about her delighted him. Occasionally, he'd delved into her memories, and most of them infuriated him, made him want to kill anyone who had ever hurt her. He'd be doing a lot of murder, because she'd been hurt time and time again. Talia had spent most of her life feeling unwanted and unattractive. The only happy memories he'd viewed were the ones of her with her mother, and even many of those were sad near the end of her mom's life. Talia had spent most of her young life taking care of her mother during her prolonged fight with cancer, and the rest of it completely alone.

A freak.

Just the thought of that slur against his woman made him nearly insane. Talia was special, and in no way freaky. She was…perfect.

When Drew had finally taken the number of lashes that Hunter's punishment required, he was released from the bounds, his body sagging from the pain.

How the hell did Hunter manage to do this so often? No wonder he was batshit crazy.

The cell was small, hardly big enough to enclose his body. He was barely able to move, and he had to stay in a seated position.

Panic closed in as the door began to shut, his natural demon instinct balking at being closed in, four walls confining him in a tiny little space.

The door clanked shut, plunging Drew into darkness. He strained against the walls and the door unconsciously, his sole objective being relief from the pain of being confined.

A scream in his head was the only thing that made him stop fighting—Talia's shriek of pain. "Fuck! I need out. She's in trouble," he rasped in a low, frustrated voice. He pounded both fists furiously against the walls, now desperate to get to his mate.

He heard another scream, really listening this time, before coming to another conclusion. "She's not in trouble with the Evils…she's hurting." Drew knew her in ways that were frightening, and he could tell the difference between her fear and pain.

Drew! He heard her scream for the third time, now clear enough for him to make out his own name.

Drew scrambled to block his thoughts, but he wasn't able to do it. He had no magic as long as he was locked up, no way to hide his emotions from Talia.

And he realized with horror, much too late, that Talia could feel every bit of his pain.

He tried to blank his mind, to not let the pain of his imprisonment permeate his being, but his reaction was elementary, instinctively demon; he was screwed. In the end, he failed miserably, his angry, anguished demon crying out in fury and torment.

Chapter Six

rew's hurting; he's in trouble. I need to help him!
Talia bit her lip to muffle another scream, her body curled into
a fetal position on the kitchen floor.

"What's happening to her?" Kat asked Hunter, Kristoff, and Zach,
the men having just arrived at Drew's house. Kat knelt by Talia's side,
her hand stroking Talia's hair anxiously.

"I don't know," Kristoff answered, his voice gruff and concerned.

Talia's mind reached for Drew, but all she could find was misery
and sorrow, and it was tearing her apart. "Drew. He's hurting," she
murmured aloud, her body thrashing with every wave of pain he was
experiencing.

"She knows," Zach said angrily. "How the hell can that happen? They
haven't mated. And even then, she shouldn't be able to feel his pain."

"She's an empath receptive to paranormal entities," Kristoff replied
abruptly, kneeling on the floor on the other side of Talia, his hand to
her forehead and scalp. "Drew is her mate. She's connecting with him
because he can't block her right now. Fuck! I didn't know because I
didn't want to delve into her memories without permission. It shouldn't
be happening. Drew has no power right now."

"You're looking at her memories now," Hunter pointed out huskily.

"I don't have a choice," Kristoff barked, shooting a furious glance at Hunter. "I can't watch her suffer like this."

Talia could hear the droning of voices, but she was centered on Drew, and she couldn't make sense of what anybody was saying. "Help him. Please," she begged, her only thought to save Drew from his agonizing mental torture. *Why couldn't any of them help him?*

"What can we do?" Zach queried in a disturbed voice.

"What about Drew? Is there anything Irish can do?" Hunter questioned roughly.

"Drew doesn't have any power. He's imprisoned. You should know better than anyone what it's like. But I have no doubt he knows what's happening to Talia. She's psychic and they have a connection that's working even without his magic because they're mates and she's an empath. She blocks it herself most of the time, but Drew's pain reached her, even from a distance, and she opened the pathways because she knew he was in trouble," Kristoff answered abruptly.

Talia? Don't fret, mo mhuirnín. I'm fine.

Talia could hear Drew's voice in her mind, and he was far from being okay. Talia felt his desperation and despair, even though he was trying to mask it and make light of it—unsuccessfully. "You're suffering," Talia whimpered, her body shuddering.

"Are they actually communicating? And where is Drew?" Kat asked frantically, her voice panicked as she looked at Kristoff questioningly.

"He's serving Hunter's sentence," Zach answered angrily. "I knew I should have insisted. Dammit! You wouldn't have been able to feel what I was feeling because I wouldn't have had my magic. And when I do, I can block it."

Kat shot Zach a warning look that said they would discuss his comment later. "How long?" she asked curtly.

"Drew's imprisoned until dawn," Kristoff replied grimly.

"Can you put her somewhere more comfortable? I'll stay with her." Kat's voice was resigned.

"I'll stay with her," Hunter interjected. "Better yet, I'm going back and taking his place."

"You…" Kristoff said sharply. "You will leave. Once I give the order for a Sentinel to take a punishment for another, it can't be undone. Go and think about whether or not your selfish actions were worth causing your brother and an innocent pain, a human who we're duty-bound to protect. I'll deal with you later, when I'm able to be a little more rational. For now, your powers are bound." Kristoff's blue eyes glowed as he glared in Hunter's direction…and Hunter disappeared almost instantaneously.

"We'll stay with her, Kristoff," Zach told his king solemnly.

Talia felt Drew's mind drifting away from her, and the separation was more excruciating than his pain. She didn't want him to leave her. If he was going to hurt, she'd rather bear the suffering with him than be separated from him. "No," she cried out. "Don't go!"

Leave me, Talia. I'll be home soon.

Talia didn't want to leave Drew. She needed to be with him.

"What are you doing?" Kat asked in a hushed voice.

Kristoff extended his palm, centering it on the top of Talia's scalp. "Mind suspension," he answered absently, his concentration on Talia. "I need to separate her from Drew. She'll stay suspended until he returns."

Talia tried to claw at her face, the distance growing between her and Drew making her frantic. She tried to project her mind out to reach him, but suddenly, there was nothing. And then, she had no more thoughts, no more pain, as she was sucked into a void of darkness.

Her body went limp and lifeless.

"Is she still in pain? Can she still feel Drew?" Kat asked as she straightened Talia's body into a more comfortable position.

"No. She'll feel nothing until Drew returns. She'll sleep," Kristoff said sharply. "I'll transport her up to her room."

"You have some scary powers sometimes, Kristoff," Zach commented, his tone fascinated but relieved. "Kat and I will stay with her."

"I'll stay with her," Kristoff said, his voice letting Zach know he wasn't relenting.

"I made a vow," Zach argued.

"As did I." Kristoff turned his stubborn gaze to Zach.

"We'll all stay," Kat interrupted calmly. "We want to, Kristoff. Please."

Kristoff looked from Zach to Kat before nodding his approval and transporting Talia away to a more comfortable place to rest.

Zach clasped Kat's hand possessively, pulling her to her feet, and they followed moments later.

Bloody Hell!

Drew stumbled to his feet just as the sun peaked over the horizon, his brain scrambled, his whole body roaring to life as his magic returned to him slowly.

He'd been released from his cell. He was free. And the only thing he needed right now was Talia. He needed to reassure himself that she was okay, feel her softness against him to know that she was well and healthy.

She felt my pain, dammit!

The two of them had been connected last night, and he knew he hadn't imagined it. What shouldn't have been possible had really happened. He'd spoken to her, felt her presence, heard her scream, before she'd drifted away from him.

Drew dressed himself as soon as his returning magic allowed him to, questions rolling through his mind.

How had their connection been possible? They hadn't yet mated, and even then, she shouldn't have been able to feel his distress unless he allowed it, and *that* would never happen. Drew had no doubt that the light that Talia had already cast into his soul had helped him last night. The beginning had been painful, but he'd focused on the light in his soul that was Talia, and had been able to bear the pain more easily. Yeah. It had still hurt like a bitch, but it had lessened, had gotten easier when he focused on her, on her brilliance that had started to warm his soul.

I'm going to fucking kill Hunter.

For the first time since he'd met his brothers, he was actually feeling murderous toward one of them, furious that Hunter's actions, as well as his own, had caused his mate pain. He didn't give a flying fuck about his own suffering, but he wanted to tear his brother apart for making Talia hurt in *any* way.

Drew swayed for a moment, his equilibrium still off, his eyes burning like liquid flame.

I can't feel Talia. I can't feel anything from her, even with my magic coming back.

Drew paced impatiently in the courtyard, fists clenched, ignoring the penalty Sentinels who were starting to stir around the area. His power needed to settle so he could transport, and he was agitated that it was taking too damn long. It was surging, returning quickly, but it seemed like an eternity to Drew when all he wanted, all he needed, was to get to Talia.

Finally!

He felt the electric current flow through his body, and he transported straight to his house.

"Talia!" he bellowed loudly, his booming voice echoing through his enormous home as he stood at his own bedroom.

Kristoff appeared in front of him almost immediately. "She's fine, Drew."

"Not good enough. I need to see her for myself. Where is she?" Drew growled, his need for his mate almost feral.

Kristoff slapped a hand on Drew's shoulder. "Sleeping. She's well. Zach, Kat, and I watched over her all night. We promised you we would."

"I heard her scream. I felt her with me," Drew said, confused. It wasn't an illusion. He knew it wasn't.

"She *was* with you for a short time."

"How is that possible?" Drew shook off Kristoff's grip and paced the bedroom like an angry lion, wanting nothing more than to see Talia. But he needed to understand what was happening—for her sake. How could he protect her if he didn't understand what was going on?

"Talia's an empath. She doesn't just see otherworldly entities. She experiences their emotions." Kristoff's face was grim. "But she blocks it most of the time. Somehow you two connected through her own abilities and not yours."

"How do you know that?" Drew swung around and shot Kristoff an angry glance.

"I invaded her memories. I didn't have much choice. I had to know why she could feel you so I could stop her pain."

Drew shuddered, the thought of anyone other than him having access to his woman's mind making his possessive instincts roar to life. Rationally, he tried to suppress them. Having Kristoff search Talia's mind was better than her experiencing his pain. Still, it rankled. Drew had seen some of Talia's memories, but he'd never focused on that. Shit! "What did you do to her?"

"She'll be waking shortly. I put her in mind suspension. It's not much different than magically induced sleep. It blanked her mind so she couldn't feel your pain. Once she wakes and you're there and out of pain, the door to her pathway should close automatically."

"You can do that?" Drew asked, surprised.

"Yes," Kristoff answered evasively. "Obviously I can."

Drew dropped the topic, more interested in his woman. "Bring her here to me," Drew demanded, wanting Talia in his bed. He needed to see her, and he wanted her in his bed when she woke.

Kristoff's eyes glowed briefly and Talia appeared in the middle of Drew's bed, clearly still clothed in last night's jeans and a lightweight sweater. Zach and Kat came running into the room with alarmed expressions, seconds after Talia appeared.

"Leave us," Drew growled, his patience at an end. He didn't want anyone else near Talia right now. After an endless night of worrying about whether or not she was okay, he felt nearly feral at the sight of her sleeping in his bed.

Mine!

He fought to control his animalistic reactions, his need to soothe her almost as strong as his need to fuck her. Actually, the two needs were so entwined it was hard to tell which one he wanted more. His demon instincts had been leashed for too long, and they wouldn't be denied much longer. He wanted his mate, and there was very little that was going to stop him from having her. The connection he'd had with her the night before, the pain she'd suffered because of him, had made him come undone.

He never saw Kristoff, Zach, and Kat leave. The only thing consuming him at that moment was Talia.

She moaned as he stalked toward the bed, her body awakening from her induced sleep. Just that needy little sound stirred up images of her moaning beneath him, calling his name, begging him to fuck her.

Bloody hell! His self-control was exhausted as he climbed onto the bed.

Talia woke to the most tantalizing scent she'd ever experienced: the mouthwatering scent of Drew. She knew his smell, and it filled her nostrils and lit her body on fire as she turned her head and buried her face in her pillow. "Drew," she murmured softly, trying to clear her foggy brain. Something had happened…

"Oh, God…Drew!" Her eyes flew open in panic as her memory returned abruptly.

Drew…in pain and helpless.

Drew…trying to send her away to protect her.

And then…nothing. Everything was a blank after she had experienced Drew's pain and he had drifted out of reach of her senses.

Talia sat up quickly, her body never reaching a complete sitting position. It balked after running into an immovable, hot, and fierce-looking obstruction.

Drew.

Her entire being flooded with relief, and her eyes darted over him, looking for any sign of discomfort. The only thing she saw embedded in the glowing amber of his eyes was pure, raw desire. She wrapped her arms around him and threw herself into his embrace, her only solace feeling him well, whole, and away from the torment of last night. "What happened?" she asked him tremulously as she stroked his muscular back, and threaded her fingers through his hair, still trying to assure herself that he was really okay. "I was so afraid for you."

Drew held her tight and rocked her, his voice husky in her ear. "I'm fine, *mo chridhe.* I had to serve a penalty for an infraction. I didn't know we'd connect like that."

Talia pulled away from him in surprise, her head lowering back to the pillow. "You broke Sentinel rules?" Drew loved being a Sentinel, and somehow she couldn't see him stepping out of bounds in his duty.

"Hunter," Drew answered angrily. "He's killing himself. He's walking a very fine line with his sanity right now. I took his punishment for killing Evils without being provoked. It's my right. He's too close to the edge. But had I known what would happen, that you would suffer with me, I wouldn't have done it."

Talia couldn't keep her outrage in check. Drew had suffered for someone else's crimes? She'd sensed Hunter's confusion and pain, and even his battle to keep his sanity, but this was too damn much. "Bastard. I'll knee him hard enough to put his balls in his throat," she vowed furiously, the memory of what Drew had experienced because of his brother's actions driving her anger. Drew was a natural protector, taking care of whoever needed it. The problem was…who was protecting Drew? Talia decided it was her job to watch out for him, since he stubbornly wouldn't stop protecting everyone else.

Drew barked out a laugh as he pinned her hands over her head. "My fierce little protector," he answered, his tone gruff but slightly amused. "Stay away from Hunter. Stay away from any other male right now, but especially Hunter. He's not stable."

Talia's irritation faded away as she watched Drew's glowing eyes, mesmerized. His jaw was clenched and a bead of sweat ran down his face, his breathing so ragged that she would have sworn he'd just run a marathon.

He wants me. He wants me as much as I want him.

Although she knew he desired her because of the mating instinct, she had never seen him quite this untamed, and his emotions were battering at her because she'd let him in last night, and that door hadn't quite closed yet. Mating instinct or not, she wanted him, and his wild, unruly passion was making her insane, his desire feeding her own. "I still can't believe you actually want me. I'm a history geek. Why was I chosen as your mate? I still don't understand."

"I have no fucking idea, *mo grha*. But you complete me like no other ever could, and I don't just want you…I need you. I crave you with every cell in my body." His voice was low and guttural as he continued. "I'm a poor Irish peasant with nothing to recommend me. I couldn't even read until I became a Sentinel. I have nothing to make me worthy of a woman like you, but I still need you. I don't think I can live without you, Talia." He took a deep breath and demanded, "I know you can sense my emotions. Read me. Know exactly how I feel."

Talia shook her head slowly and closed her eyes. "I can't," she told him desperately, letting the door on her empath abilities close. "I've worked for a very long time to block my senses and I'm already losing my control with you. It hurts too much; I experience too much." If she let her ability completely loose, she was afraid it would consume her. She'd spent too many years being a prisoner of her emotions, letting the pain of spirits and other entities nearly drive her mad. Although she was fairly certain she could still block other entities, it was Drew she feared the most. Opening completely to him in addition to what she was already feeling would be likely to burn her alive.

"You already opened yourself to me last night," Drew reminded her, lowering his head to let his lips explore the sensitive skin at the side of her neck, and working his way up to the tender flesh of her ear, biting gently at her earlobe. "Feel me, Talia. I swear you'll experience nothing but pleasure. I'll sate you until you beg for mercy. I feel your need, and I have to make you come right now. I can't take this anymore."

Talia melted as she met his eyes once more, the flames in the glowing amber orbs her undoing. "I don't need to feel you any more than I already do, Drew. I already feel more than I can handle. I need you so much. Please."

She was done waiting, and as his head swooped down to claim her mouth, she knew Drew was about to become the lover she'd never had, but had always dreamed of in her most private fantasies. He'd strip her bare, literally and physically, and finally, she welcomed it.

Talia was done asking questions, wondering why Drew wanted her. It only mattered that he did, and that he made her feel beautiful and desired. Finally, she was ready to be brave instead of hiding away, to reach out and take what she really needed and embrace her fate.

Chapter Seven

For once in her life, Talia willingly released herself into another's care, letting herself experience every sensation that Drew was giving her.

She started as she suddenly felt them skin-to-skin, Drew's cock heavy and hard against her thigh. "We're naked," she sighed, luxuriating in the sensual feel of his hot, muscular body sliding against hers.

"My demon is demanding I fuck you, *mo grha*, and I don't have the patience for niceties this time. But next time..." he growled.

Talia's already flooded pussy became even more drenched, her need becoming increasingly urgent. Drew finally released his hold on her wrists, and she wrapped her arms around his shoulders, her short nails biting into his skin as he devoured her. There was no other explanation for what he was doing with his mouth and tongue, the way he was tasting her skin with small nips of his teeth and then a lave of his rough tongue as he moved down her neck and into the valley between her breasts. It was as though he was trying to brand her as his—every inch of her—and it was working. She moaned as he bit a nipple, the pleasure/pain exploding inside her belly, the warmth spreading to every inch of her body as his tongue followed the bite, soothing her stinging nipple with his tongue. He tormented her by repeating his action over and over, switching from breast to breast, until Talia was ready to lose her mind. "Please," she begged, not even really sure what she wanted as he moved down her abdomen.

Drew looked up at her, his eyes almost feral. "Has any man ever made you come, Talia?" His voice was tight and low, as though it were difficult for him to ask.

Talia could feel his raw sense of possession. "No," she whispered honestly. Her one experience in early adulthood hadn't been anything other than awkward, fast, and painful.

"Don't think about him. Don't ever think about him," Drew snarled, moving between her thighs and opening her to him. He pushed her knees up, spreading her almost painfully wide. "This is mine," he declared gruffly, staking his claim greedily as he trailed an index finger over her breast and down her stomach. "This is mine." His palm went to her thigh, running roughly up and down the sensitive skin. "All of you is mine." He groaned as his fingers delved into her pussy, meeting only wet heat. "Fuck!" His big body shuddered as he slid a finger inside her channel. "You're tight and so wet, Talia. For me. Only for me," he declared ferociously, removing his finger and bringing it in slow, sensual circles up to her clit.

He watched her face as his finger moved, teasing the sensitive bundle of nerves until her whole body shook with need. His gaze ran up and down her body, his expression carnal as he tormented her, their eyes finally meeting in a clash of desire. "You're beautiful. So beautiful like this," Drew said huskily, reaching a hand out to palm her breast, pinching her nipple so exquisitely that every nerve in her body reacted.

A whimper escaped her mouth, and her hips rose up, begging him to put her out of her misery. Her entire body was flushed with desire, and all she wanted was to feel him inside her, joining them together. "I need you," she moaned. "Please, Drew." His teasing was killing her. She could feel his need to dominate his mate, and she yielded to him, her arousal peaking even further as she looked at his powerful form towering above her, his only thought to pleasure her and make her his.

"You'll come for me, Talia." It wasn't a question...it was a command. Drew released her breast and she wanted to cry out in protest as his finger left her clit.

She felt the heat of his mouth on her core almost immediately and she cried out his name in sweet relief as she felt his mouth feasting on her pussy. She relished his urgency. She melted at his frenzied consuming of the liquid heat created by his tongue lapping eagerly between her folds, his hunger seemingly insatiable, as though she were the best thing he'd ever tasted.

Talia speared her fingers into his hair, her grip tight on his skull. God, the feel of him was enthralling, the pleasure so intense that she was vibrating with desire. "Make me come, Drew. Please." Her back arched in pleasure and frustration as his tongue slid roughly over her clit, again and again, bringing her higher and higher.

He complied, giving her the pressure she needed to fly outside of herself, the spiral of hot sensations starting in her belly and curling outward until Talia felt herself trembling in the throes of a climax so powerful that she couldn't do anything but let it take her over. "Drew. Oh God, Drew," she moaned, feeling like he'd just incinerated her.

He reared up, his expression fierce and savage as he looked at her. "Need to fuck you, Talia. No control left," he rasped, his amber eyes shooting sparks around them.

"Yes," she panted, needing to feel him inside her more than she needed her next breath. Her desire was that all-consuming, her need to be joined with him as elemental as his.

He brought his cock to the opening of her hungry, clenching channel, watching as it slid inside her, hissing as he viewed their joining. Drew looked mesmerized, and he released a grunt of male satisfaction as he buried himself balls deep inside her.

Talia couldn't say that she didn't feel stretched to her limit, and there was a moment of pain because it had been so long and Drew was built so big. But the feel of him inside her eclipsed everything else, the pleasure almost unbearable. Drew filled her, made her feel like the most desirable woman on the planet.

Lowering his body over hers, he said hoarsely, "You *are* the most desirable woman on the planet. You're it for me." He took her mouth as his hips flexed, pulling back until he was almost out of her and driving back in with a forceful thrust. "I've never known this kind of hunger until

I met you. I crave you, Talia. And fucking you is the most satisfying thing I've ever done."

Talia moaned into his embrace, wrapping her arms around his back and putting her legs around his waist, urging him on. She could feel his desperation, and she wanted his unrestrained possession, this rough claiming. Nothing else would do for either of them. His tongue moved inside her mouth, owning her with the same relentless rhythm as his cock. Slick with perspiration, they strained together, their bodies entwining until it was hard to know where one ended and the other began.

He released her mouth with a low groan, his cock still pummeling into her, each thrust more demanding and primal. "Come apart for me, Talia. I want to watch you take your pleasure this time. Take it from me. Only from me," Drew demanded, his tone dominant and graveled, his eyes covetous and wild as he watched her face.

Talia moaned, his words inflaming her, and trembled as he changed positions, grinding against her mound with every stroke of his cock. She met every pump of his hips with an uncontrolled desperation of her own, needing to make him orgasm as badly as she needed it herself. Their desires were intertwined, and it was difficult to separate one from the other, but it didn't really matter. Some of their needs were mirror images of the other's, all of them soul deep and primal.

With a cry of sweet release, she climaxed violently, helplessly, as Drew stared down at her, groaning in male satisfaction as he continued to fill her over and over with unrelenting strokes. Then, he threw his head back and groaned, the muscles in his neck straining as he let go and flooded her with his hot release.

Talia panted as she gazed at him, knowing that watching him right here, right now, was the most amazingly beautiful, hottest thing she'd ever seen. Muscles clenched, his powerful body shuddered as his animalistic groan reverberated through the room. Sweat trickled down his chest and abdomen, and it made his golden skin shimmer. Talia knew the image was branded into her memory, and she was glad. She never wanted to forget this moment in time.

Drew rolled to his side and pulled her over him with a growl. "You nearly killed me, *mo chridhe*. And you're going to see me come a lot more in the future. No need to keep the memory when it'll just keep getting better and better. And I'm not all that attractive," he told her in a low and slightly melancholy tone, his hands stroking her ass and back lovingly as she rested, completely sated, on top of him.

Her heart still pounding furiously, she told him breathlessly, "Are you kidding? You're every woman's most lusty wet dream."

"Am I, now?" he answered in an amused voice, his brogue heavy during this unguarded, intimate moment. "Now that would be a waste, really. The only woman I want to attract is you."

Talia's heart squeezed, making it even harder to recover her breath. Drew was so incredibly hot, and heartrendingly sweet. "There isn't a woman in the world who wouldn't drool over you. How can you say you aren't the hottest male in the universe?"

Drew shrugged. "What's so attractive about an Irish peasant? Believe me, at one time I wasn't a pretty sight."

"Does becoming a Sentinel alter your physical appearance?" she asked curiously.

"Not really. But it made me a hell of a lot more healthy," he answered in a falsely nonchalant voice.

Talia hit him playfully on the shoulder. "Then you were always a hottie. You were just malnourished." Again, the thought of Drew starving nearly broke her heart.

"I did manual labor. I was old before my time," Drew commented. "And I wasn't much to look at to begin with."

Talia pulled back and gaped at him. "You're gorgeous, Drew. The most handsome man I've ever seen."

"I don't think so. Maybe it's the mating instinct that makes you think so," he remarked casually.

"It is not. I might not be wearing my glasses, but I can still see you." There wasn't a single thing that she didn't find appealing in Drew, mating instinct or not. Well...except maybe his occasional stubbornness wasn't particularly pleasant at times, but she even liked that because it was probably what had gotten him through the Great Famine alive.

"Ditto," Drew drawled low and husky. He put his hands on both sides of her face, making her meet his compelling gaze. "Why is it so hard to believe that I see you the same way? I love the fact that you're tall, and have the most amazingly sexy legs that seem to go on forever. Your eyes are so beautiful I want to drown in them. And you have the body of a goddess. You're so intelligent that I want to worship your mind, and I don't feel worthy of you." Drew let out an exasperated sigh. "Still, you're the most beautiful thing I've ever seen in my human life and in my years as a Sentinel, and I'll do everything in my power to make you mine and keep you safe. I need you. And I think you need me, too. If anything, I think you got the raw end of the deal, and if I were a better man, I'd somehow let you go, but I can't."

A lone tear flowed down Talia's cheek. It was humbling how much this glorious man wanted her. "I've never had anybody, Drew. Not since my mom died."

He kissed the tear away and told her huskily, "Neither have I, *mo grha*. But now that I know what it's like to have you as mine, I can't give you up. Please don't ever ask me to. I'm not sure I'd survive it. I want to be yours, Talia. I want to be there when you're sad, when you're happy, when you need me—which I fucking hope is all the time. I want your face to be the last thing I see every night and the first thing I'm lucky enough to see in the morning. I want to make up for every moment you've been alone by filling your life with so much happiness that you'll forget anything that happened before we met." He paused, his voice going from sensually persuasive to agitated. "But I still want to kill the bastards who hurt you."

Talia let out a startled laugh. A few more tears were dotting her cheeks at Drew's heartfelt declaration. Trust Drew to mix up what *was* a very sweet speech with a murderous intent at the end of it. But her heart was still singing because everything he said was all for her. Even the homicidal comment was revenge for slights toward her.

She reached up and touched his cheek, her hand trembling slightly. God, but this stubborn, dominant Irishman moved her, especially now, when he was vulnerable, because she was certain no one else ever saw that part of him. "I love the way you make me feel." Talia stroked his jawline, loving the feel of his whiskered, abrasive skin underneath her fingertips. "I've never felt like anything except a freak. Suddenly, I feel like a desirable woman, some kind of seductress."

"You don't need to be a seductress. My cock gets hard just from thinking about you," Drew mumbled.

Talia rubbed sensually against him, feeling his member already hard and hot against her thigh. Kat was right. Didn't a Sentinel ever get tired?

"You're pushing your luck, woman. You're already going to be sore tomorrow," Drew warned.

"I thought I'd try out my newfound sexuality." She wriggled on top of him, loving the feel of his rock-hard body beneath her. "Maybe I can arouse you this time."

Talia found herself pinned to the bed before she could blink, Drew's marvelously massive bulk on top of her.

"No need. I'm already there," he growled, aggressively taking her mouth with his.

Okay, maybe Sentinels required very little seduction, and as he continued to ravish her, she didn't think that was necessarily a bad thing.

The next morning, Talia actually *was* sore in muscles that she hadn't even known she had. But she didn't care.

"Why didn't you tell me you were an empath?" Drew asked curiously as he devoured the largest breakfast Talia had ever seen.

He'd taken her out to a cozy little place that was apparently well-known for its breakfast menu and they were currently tucked away in a quiet booth. Drew was consuming almost everything on the table with obvious abandon, everything except for her food. Lowering her eyes to occupy herself with buttering her toast, she answered, "I learned to block it. I don't really notice it anymore."

"Then how did you feel my pain?"

Talia had been asking herself the same question. "I don't know. It's strange. That's never happened unless the entity is actually in my presence. Can it be the mate connection?"

He crammed another piece of bacon in his mouth, chewing thoughtfully before answering, "Very likely. Mates like you and Kat are unknown to us, completely different from anything we've ever seen before. There are so many unanswered questions. I don't like it."

Tilting her head to look at him, she asked, "Why?"

"I want you for my mate, Talia. I intend to talk you into accepting me. But I don't like not knowing what will happen. What if the dormant power actually hurts you? It would kill me if mating with me harmed you in any way," he answered unhappily.

"It didn't kill Kat. Drew, I think there's a reason for the change in the Sentinel mates, at least for you and Zach, something bigger than just a fluke. You told me the Evils are getting more powerful, doing things they've never done before. I think some of the *radiants* are meant to be, that they're part of a bigger picture. If the balance is tipping toward the Evils, then it has to be righted somehow."

Drew shot her a surprised look. "I don't think any of us have ever thought about it that way, except possibly Kristoff, and he's not talking. How do you think it's all connected?"

Talia warmed at the fact that Drew really listened to her, valued her opinions. She'd never really had anyone to talk to before who really listened without going cross-eyed from boredom when she got on one of her theories. Well...except for Pumpkin, but Talia was pretty sure her cat just tolerated her babbling. "I'm not sure, but I think it has to do with the balance of power. The gods created both the Evils and the Sentinels so there would be stasis, equal good and evil. If that harmony is lost and the power is tilting toward the Evils, there has to be something—or some people—to return everything to the former state of equilibrium." She paused before asking excitedly , "Are there any demon prophecies?"

Drew gave her a curious look. "You believe in prophecies?"

Talia took a sip of her coffee before answering. "Obviously I believe in facts and science, but everything I've studied never included gods and demons, ghosts and spirits—or they were only considered to be myth. If I know that all of those things really exist, I see no reason not to believe in prophecies. I'm a scholar, Drew. I've seen the evidence. I can't deny this all exists just because I've been taught differently. The spirits and ghosts I've known about since I was a child, but the demon and gods thing really shook up my world. My specialty is ancient Greek history. I looked at mythology as folklore and legends. How was I to know that they really existed?"

"And now?" Drew urged.

"Now I know they do, and I guess I'm going to have to learn to live in a bigger world." Talia sighed. "Everything I know isn't all black and white. I don't know why I have the compulsions to learn about demons, but they're very real."

Drew studied her, his expression alarmed. "You're still having them?"

"No," she answered hurriedly. "I'm living with a walking, talking demon history encyclopedia," she teased him softly. "The compulsions are gone. But I know they happened, and I know I had no control over them."

Talia abruptly stopped talking, her body first stilling and then shuddering as she felt the presence of evil...big, bad Evils. "Incoming powerful Evils," she warned Drew urgently, dropping her fork so fast that it landed with a loud clank on her plate.

Drew had already gotten his wallet out, ready to pay the bill. He dropped a handful of bills on the table, grabbed her hand a second later, and flashed them out of the restaurant.

Moments later, two large elder Evils with glowing red eyes arrived, eyes darting around the restaurant, their expressions frustrated that Drew and Talia had eluded them again.

Summoned by Drew, a group of warrior Sentinels appeared. Bound by a different set of rules, they were able to engage in battle, but there were casualties, and plenty of them on the Sentinel side. Although the Evils were outnumbered, they were more powerful than several warriors put together.

The elder Evils made no attempt to hide who and what they were, or the fact that they were very unhappy about losing their prey. The few customers and employees who saw the demons tried to run past the gory battle to get to the door and escape. One or two of the customers never made it.

The warrior Sentinels finally drove the two Evils back to the demon realm, but their hearts were heavy as they took their wounded and dead, and set about cleaning up the mess the Evils had made.

Chapter Eight

$\mathcal{K}$ ristoff paced the goddess Athena's enormous solarium, totally oblivious that he was destroying several of the delicate green leaves, his big body colliding with the plants as he moved back and forth across the dirt floor, frustrated. "Goran's out of control. My warrior Sentinels all over the world are battling Evils that are slaughtering humans, and that aren't turning to dust from breaking the rules here in the human realm. It's not possible for them to have become powerful enough to do that," Kristoff muttered angrily, worried about the future of his Sentinels for the first time in thousands of years.

Athena frowned thoughtfully as she saw small sections of her plants breaking apart as Kristoff plowed past them. "The balance of power is shifting in their favor, but the Sentinels will equal it again," she answered, crossing her legs delicately beneath a crimson silk gown, sipping her tea at a small patio table as she watched the Sentinel king move restlessly through the indoor garden. "We knew this day would come, Kristoff."

Yes. He knew. He'd always known. But damned if he knew exactly how everything was going to go down, and it irked the shit out of him. He'd been aware, since the Great War and the dawn of the Sentinels, that there would come a time when evil would tip the scales in its favor, but he didn't have to like it. "It hasn't been this uneven since we fought the Great War and fought back the Evils after they overran the Earth. The covenants have held."

"The gods' powers have slowly waned, and the Evils have the advantage now. The elders are sucking power from the *radiant* females they've been holding over the years, in particular one female more powerful than all the others," Athena told Kristoff, watching him over the rim of her cup.

"I know that. Those women don't lose their soul and die in the demon realm. They regenerate because they're intended mates for Sentinels. And the Evils' energy is more powerful than sucking souls from millions of humans, simply by feeding constantly from those women." Kristoff's big body shuddered in anger at the thought of human Sentinel *radiants* being held captive by the Evils. "Are they all like Kat and Talia?" Kristoff asked Athena, his voice cracking with emotion.

"Only one. The others are normal *radiants*," Athena answered vaguely. "The only mates who can regenerate in the demon realm are the ones who were never mated with their Sentinel, and they're capable of it because they still retain their power. It's never been released."

Kristoff cursed and stopped pacing, throwing himself into a too-small-for-his-body chair across from Athena. Dammit! Every one of those women had unknowingly made a bargain with the Evils, and he had no way to rescue them without causing a major disaster of epic proportions. If he were to try to take the women from the demon realm while they were under an Evil bargain, it would not only tip the scales of balance, but possibly destroy mankind because he'd broken a critical covenant. While the Evils' creators were gone, the Sentinels were elementally connected to Athena, and she was still very much alive, and needed to stay that way. For a Sentinel, breaking rules in the demon realm came with a much larger penalty than death. It would stretch out to the humans, allowing the Evils to do more heinous things in the Sentinels' realm, the human realm. "Shit. We're so screwed," Kristoff muttered furiously.

"No we're not," Athena snapped hotly. "Read the prophecies, Kristoff. Maybe we don't know exactly how it ends, but there's a solution, a way out." A scroll appeared in her hand, and she handed it to Kristoff. "We just need to dust the little bastards," she decided vehemently.

Kristoff accepted the scroll from Athena while stifling a laugh. "More television?" he asked, noticing that Athena was using contemporary American expressions more and more.

"It's boring here." She shrugged her delicate shoulders. "A woman does what she can to keep from going crazy from the isolation."

Athena wasn't exactly a woman—she was a goddess—but Kristoff wasn't about to remind her of that. The truth was, she *was* isolated in this uninhabited area of the Olympic Peninsula and hadn't seen another soul except him for thousands of years. "I'll study them again," he answered, gesturing to the scroll to make Athena feel better. He knew the prophecies by heart, but the Fates were real bitches to understand sometimes. Most of what was written could have many different meanings. "There has to be an answer." There had better be, because he wasn't about to see his Sentinels destroyed and the Earth ravaged as it had been when the Evils ruled the Earth. Every Sentinel had a drive to protect human life, and his was greater than the others. It was his duty, his purpose.

"My Sentinels won't fail me, Kristoff. You won't fail me," she murmured, her voice not wavering.

Kristoff felt his gut clench, hoping Athena was right. The goddess had given him back his life, and he'd rather die than fail her. "No, I won't," he agreed, brushing off all thought of failure. It wasn't an option. Too much relied on him and the Sentinels doing what they were created to do.

Athena worried her long, very blonde braid that hung over her shoulder, stroking the tail of it thoughtfully. "Hunter is getting very close to the edge. Send him to me," she demanded quietly. "I can help him."

Kristoff stared at Athena, dumbfounded. "I bound his powers. He may already be beyond saving," he answered, his voice vibrating with sorrow. "How can he find you? And why him? You haven't ever wanted to see another one of the Sentinels before." Hell, if Athena could help Hunter, he was all for it. But she'd never mentioned the possibility of intervening in the past. She left all Sentinel communication to him. "He's damaged, Athena."

She raised a blonde eyebrow at him questioningly. "You actually think he could hurt me?"

Kristoff barked out a humorless laugh. Hell, no. Athena was a goddess, even though her powers were limited. She might look like a blonde angel, but she could kick Hunter's ass in a heartbeat. "No," he answered aloud. "I'm more worried about Hunter pissing you off."

"I can hold my temper, Kristoff. I'm not arrogant enough to believe that I'm invincible, and I don't feel the need to rule the Earth. I just want to help the Sentinels. Send him."

His goddess had commanded, and he'd obey. "Just don't kill him. He might be a major asshole, but he's still one of my men," Kristoff requested. "How will he find you? Do you want me to transport him?"

Athena shook her head. "Just give him my location, transfer the information to him. He'll find me."

"Would you like to give me any more clues about why you even want him here?" Kristoff already had enough things that he didn't know. He'd really like to be clued in on why Athena wanted Hunter in her invisible palace and how the hell he was even going to get here.

"He needs to be healed. That's all I know right now. And he needs to enter my territory willingly."

Athena looked agitated, and Kristoff knew that she had moments when she wasn't all-knowing, even though she was a goddess. Information came to her like it came to him…in too damn small amounts, and only when it was time. "I'll send him." Rising to his feet, he added, "I've got to go. Things are going south pretty fast."

Athena got to her feet gracefully. "I have one more thing I have to tell you before you leave, something that might come as rather a shock," she said gravely. "I would have told you before, but I didn't know until today."

"Yeah?" Kristoff answered guardedly, his voice graveled. She was a goddess and he was a demon king. He wasn't sure what Athena could actually say to surprise him.

But he was so wrong. So very wrong. Athena managed to drop a bomb on him that knocked his whole world off its axis. He left her presence, still stunned and shaken, knowing his world would never be quite the same.

Talia landed on top of Drew in unfamiliar surroundings, her brain completely scrambled.

Obviously Drew had slowed down his transport from the restaurant enough that she was still conscious, but fast enough that she was pretty damn dizzy. She sat up slowly, her head spinning, straddling Drew as she ran a hand through her hair to push it back impatiently, moving the blinding curtain from her face.

"You okay, love?"

The husky baritone came from beneath her, and her eyes flew to Drew's concerned face. "Yeah. I think so." She put her hands on his chest to get her balance. "Where are we?"

"Kristoff's house. I'm not sure my place is safe anymore." He sat up, holding her straddled across his lap. "Kristoff's home is warded with better security. He only leaves it open to a few of his Sentinels."

Talia assumed the Winston brothers were three of those Sentinels allowed unrestricted access to Kristoff's home. "Are the people in the restaurant in danger?"

"I summoned the warriors to come there as soon as you felt the presence of Evils. Rescue Sentinels are only allowed to fight in self-defense, which is why Hunter is in trouble so damn much. The warriors can engage in battle if they feel an Evil's intent to harm. They'll do their best to drive the Evils back to the demon realm where they belong," Drew replied, his voice grave.

"How do you fight the Evils? Obviously you've had conflicts," Talia queried curiously.

"I let them take one shot at me, and that's all they get," Drew answered gruffly. "Once they try to kill me or harm a human, they're fair game."

Somehow it didn't seem fair that a rescue Sentinel couldn't defend himself until an Evil attempted to behead him, and Talia told Drew just that.

"It's the rules. Every Sentinel has a purpose and his own set of rules. We rescue humans from themselves. For the most part, rescue Sentinels are strong enough that regular Evils don't tangle with us. But I appreciate your concern, *mo chridhe*," he told her, amused.

"So you can summon other Sentinels?" Talia asked, still not happy that some Evil could try to behead Drew before he could defend himself.

"Only in an emergency, when another type of Sentinel is needed. An official summons can be sent to other types of Sentinels. I can't summon one of my own kind," Drew answered glumly. "If that were possible, I'd be summoning Hunter's ass every minute so he'd stay out of trouble."

He grasped her hips as she tried to slide from his body, keeping her positioned exactly where she was. "Stay," he requested, part demanding and part pleading with her.

Talia's head was starting to clear, but Drew's proximity made her feel intoxicated, the masculine, musky scent of him enough to make her want him all over again. Her breath caught as her eyes met his, the light amber glow enthralling her. Her panties grew wet and she wriggled against his long, hard length, needing him possibly even more than she had the night before. Images from the previous day exploded in her mind, visions of pleasure like she'd never known before. It wasn't just her desire for a handsome male like Drew; it was the way he made *her* feel beautiful. His intense possessiveness and protectiveness, traits she would have thought would be off-putting, were actually the sexiest things she'd ever seen. And it made her want to own him, own his desire as badly as he seemed to want hers. The fact that he needed her with a desperation that bordered on insanity was breathtaking. "C-can we stay here?" she asked nervously, watching as his face grew more and more intense.

"Yes. Kristoff would want it if we were in danger." Drew's voice was husky and hungry, and it didn't look like his appetite was for a chocolate truffle. "If you don't stop imagining those dirty little things in your head, you're going to be experiencing them momentarily."

His words were a dark, sensual threat, and Talia felt her entire body start to tremble with longing.

Damn. Will I ever stop wanting him the moment he's close, the instant he touches me or looks at me?

Frankly, she doubted it. Drew emanated carnal, fierce desire when he looked at her, and Talia didn't think there would ever be a time that she wouldn't respond immediately to the intensity of his gaze, the way he smelled, his naughty little words. Drew Winston was everything she'd always needed, even though she'd never recognized the longing in her heart and soul for such a man until he'd opened the floodgates. And only Drew had been capable of doing it. "I waited so long for you," she murmured, unable to keep her emotions leashed.

"Not nearly as long as I waited for you, *mo grha*," he growled, his nimble fingers unbuttoning her lightweight sweater to get to her flesh. The buttons popped as he grew impatient and ripped the garment open, tore the front of her bra in half and buried his face in her chest.

Talia cried out in relief as Drew ravaged her breasts, taking the hard, sensitive nipples into his mouth and sucking, bringing both of them to painful peaks. She leaned her head back with a moan that she barely recognized as her own as his large hands cupped her ass and pulled her wet core tightly against him, the denim between them an irritating barrier to what she really needed. Drew pillaged, and Talia responded with an elemental carnality that was overwhelming.

Her fingers speared through his hair, urging him faster, harder. His emotions were beating at her and suddenly, the door to her empath ability opened to Drew, and his ferocious hunger for her nearly made her come undone, as it roared through her body with a strength that would have knocked her sideways if he hadn't been palming her ass to keep her in place. "Oh, God. Drew. I need you to fuck me right now." She clawed at his buttoned-down shirt, popping the fastenings to get to his bare skin. "Mine," she declared in a possessive, sultry voice as her fingers met the smooth, heated skin of his ripped chest. But it wasn't enough. Not nearly enough. Her short nails dug into him, needing to mark him as her own. As Drew groaned against her breast, Talia nipped at his shoulder, the need to claim him overpowering her.

I'm feeling Drew's emotions.

Yet...they weren't. They were an extension of her own need. She'd opened herself to Drew, exposing herself to the innate desire of their souls to bind, and it was damn near excruciating. It was an insatiable, overwhelming drive to mate. And now that the door had swung wide open, she was unable or unwilling to close it again.

Drew had them both naked in a heartbeat, his strong hands lifting her off his lap and onto her knees. The floor was a gleaming wood, and it was hard, but Talia never noticed. "Now, Drew." If she didn't feel him inside her in the next few seconds, she thought she was going to die from unsated longing.

"Easy, *mo chridhe*," Drew crooned softly in her ear as he covered her body with his, his chest against her back. He moved her hair aside and bit gently at the back of her neck, making Talia whimper in her need for him to mark her.

"I feel you, Drew. I feel us. Please," she begged, not comprehending how Drew managed to live with this kind of erotic torture.

"I'll give you what you need, Talia," he answered gruffly, straightening, running a palm soothingly along her back.

His fingers delved between her thighs, and he let out a strangled groan. "Bloody hell. I can't wait. You're so ready for me right now."

"Yes," she said eagerly. "Yes."

Drew impaled her in one smooth stroke, a thrust that left her breathless and sighing with the sheer bliss of feeling him buried inside her.

"No control," Drew warned, his breath heaving as he pulled back and slammed into her again, his groin meeting her ass with a satisfying slap.

"I don't care," Talia panted. She wanted it rough and possessive, fast and furious. Nothing else would do for her right now, and she knew Drew needed the same thing. This animalistic joining was the only thing that would help either one of them now.

As Drew hammered into her with a driving force that slid her forward on the slick wood, all she could think about was the fact that she felt like she was going to fly into little pieces that would burst into flames. White-hot fire pulsated through her entire body, and she lowered her head to the wood, desperately pushing back against him, meeting him stroke for stroke.

"If you're going up in flames, take me with you. We'll burn together," Drew rasped, his hands gripping her hips to hold her in place. "You're mine, Talia. My mate. I won't survive if you don't take me as yours."

His declaration was possessive, yet eloquent for a man/demon who had known very little love in his life.

As a fresh rush of heat flooded her being, Talia knew she would never reject Drew. He meant too much to her now. He was the missing piece of her soul, the bright part, even though he thought his soul was dark. "I want to be yours," Talia gasped, every nerve vibrating as she felt her impending climax. "I need to come. So bad."

"Mine! My woman to satisfy." Drew reached in front of her and stroked a hand between her thighs, finding the throbbing bundle of nerves between her wet folds. He worked her relentlessly, like a man possessed, his cock driving deep, his fingers working her slick clit until she was totally mindless.

Talia's orgasm hit her with a force that would have sent her whirling into space if Drew hadn't had her firmly in his grasp, one arm going around her waist as the force of her climax took her body over. Her channel gloved him tightly, milking his own release, ripping a tortured groan from his mouth as he buried himself inside her once more and held her tightly against him, as though he never wanted to let go.

Talia moaned as Drew straightened, pulling her limp body against him. Both of them were slick with sweat, breathing hard from the cataclysmic joining they'd both experienced. He stroked one hand across her belly while the other held her in a solid grip around her shoulders, holding them together skin-to-skin, his cock still buried inside her. "Will you really be mine?" he asked in a hoarse voice, his breath warm against her ear.

"Yes." There was nothing else to say. She wanted to be with Drew worse than anything she'd ever coveted before.

Drew sat back, turning Talia and lifting her onto his lap, frowning as he saw her reddened knees. "I hurt you." His fingers lightly traced the red areas.

Talia burst into laughter. "Like I really noticed? You just rocked my world. It was worth it."

Drew kissed her, an embrace that was so adoring, so reverent, that Talia felt her eyes begin to water. After he ended the tender intimacy of his lips languorously exploring hers, he whispered huskily , "I'll make sure you're never sorry."

Talia's heart squeezed inside her chest, aching for Drew because this was one of his vulnerable moments, a time when he didn't feel he deserved happiness. "I'll never be sorry, Drew. You've made me happier than I ever thought I could be."

Suddenly, both of them jumped as they heard a rumble that sounded like it had started beneath them and was moving closer and closer.

Drew dressed them with his magic, helping Talia to her feet. For the first time, she noticed that they were actually in a bedroom, a grand bed right across the room. Despite her alarm, she was hit by the irony that they'd just used the floor when such an enormous bed stood so close.

He wrapped his arms around her, and Talia reached out with her senses, trying to identify the roar vibrating through the house. She closed the door on her empath abilities and just tried to…feel.

It took Talia precious seconds to realize what the deafening noise really was. "Evils! I can feel their underlying presence. They're trying to mask themselves by creating a diversion—"

Her alarm turned to all-out panic, but before she could finish voicing her suspicions to Drew, she felt herself being seized by sharp claws, and she sank into instant, complete darkness, her only comfort the feel of Drew's arms still tightly around her as she succumbed.

Chapter Nine

rew had never been to the demon realm, but he knew immediately that was exactly where he and Talia had been transported. The noxious smell alone was a dead giveaway. He held his woman a little tighter, his arms tightening convulsively around her as he viewed his surroundings. They were locked in a cell, a prison that wasn't quite small enough to make him react like he did in the punishment cell, but nevertheless, it was going to be a confinement he couldn't flash his way out of. He had no power here in the demon realm, and he wasn't much different from a human as long as he remained here.

He looked down at Talia, scowling as he saw the slash on her shoulder, a mark left by the Evils. He slapped his hand over the small cut to stop the bleeding with direct pressure to the wound. It wasn't big enough to be harmful. It was a scratch, really. But his gut reaction was as strong as if they'd sliced up her whole body. One mark on her body, one second of pain, was enough to make him want to tear apart the Evil that'd left it there.

The bastards had obviously transported them quickly, fast enough that Talia was unconscious. "Assholes," he muttered fiercely, shifting her body to lay her gently on the bench, the only item in the barred prison. He lifted his hand gently from her laceration. It had stopped bleeding, but he shuddered to think about the risk of infection in this squalid atmosphere.

Striding over to the front of the enclosure, he yanked at the bars, frustrated when they didn't budge. Bloody hell! Did the whole demon realm reek as badly as the prison? He didn't see another soul—the cells next to him empty—but he could hear the wailing moans of pain coming continuously from what had to be a short distance away. They were loud and probably human, and it triggered his instinct to protect all humans, a feeling he barely noticed because he was already overwhelmed by the more powerful drive to protect his mate. He needed to get Talia away from the demon realm, and he let out an anguished snarl as he fisted the bars of their cell and shook them. They barely rattled. His strength was minimal here, nothing more than that of a regular man, and it made him nearly insane.

"Drew?" Talia's confused voice sounded weak in the large cavern where the cages were arranged.

The whole area was dimly lit, a gloomy environment that was enough to make him rush back to her and kneel beside the bench. Her eyes were open. Drew stroked her face with the back of his hand as he questioned protectively, "Are you hurting?" Kat had suffered a reaction to demon toxins when she and Zach had been attacked. They may or may not have injected them into Talia's system, and he wasn't certain he could stand to see her suffer that kind of pain.

"No," she answered more clearly, moving up into a sitting position on the bench. "What happened?"

"We're in the demon realm," Drew answered, his voice dripping with anger.

"I remember now. There was a loud noise, a diversion, and then I passed out."

"You were transported too fast."

Talia lifted her sweater to her face, breathing through the garment. "God, it stinks."

Drew wanted to tell her to breathe through her mouth, but the stench was heavy in the air, and he wasn't sure what toxins were flying around in the room. He also wasn't sure if allowing the fetid air a direct path to her lungs was such a good idea. "I know," he answered simply.

"Are we stuck here?" she asked calmly, lowering the sweater and looking straight into his eyes.

"No," Drew answered, irritated. He refused to believe they were stuck in this shithole indefinitely. He'd find a way to get her out. "I'll figure out something. But I'm powerless here, Talia, much like a human."

"Then we'll think of another way," she answered as she got up and strode to the door of their cage.

Drew marveled at the fact that Talia's mind was racing through their options and collecting data as she retrieved every bit of information she knew about the demon realm. She wasn't panicking or whining; she was trying to find a solution in that quick brain of hers. "You aren't freaking out?" he asked, unable to stop himself. Any other human, male or female, would be pissing themselves right now, and for good reason. But not his woman, and he should have known better. Her lack of fear was one of the things that scared the shit out of *him*.

"Would it help either of us if I did?" she asked reasonably. "Drew, I've dealt with paranormal entities my entire life, and I've even dealt with Evils. I can't say that I'm thrilled to be here, and yes, I'm concerned. Evils might be cunning and power-hungry, but they aren't particularly intelligent. There has to be a way to outsmart them."

"I'd rather have my powers so I could take their heads off," Drew grumbled, amazed by Talia's incredible composure.

This was the woman who was chosen as his mate. Not only was she beautiful, smart, and talented, but she was also fearless in the face of adversity. And he felt humbled once again by what fate had given him, a gift he didn't think he deserved, but one he wanted with every fiber of his being. And she wanted him as well. What a lucky bastard he was. Now, if he could just get Talia the fuck out of this hellish place. "I don't get how they even got us here. It shouldn't be possible," he contemplated. "They need a bargain to take you, and they can't bring Sentinels here. They can only kill them in the human realm. They're limited by rules, fewer rules than Sentinels, but they still have a few that are unbreakable."

"But they're evolving just like the Sentinels. They must be. They're powerful. I can sense it when they get close enough for me to feel them," Talia answered, turning to face Drew.

"The elders are more powerful than the others. The Evils you dealt with aren't elders. The elders rarely leave the demon realm." But they *had* left when they came to the human realm to attack Kat. Drew and his brothers knew the rules were changing; they just weren't sure why.

Talia started as the door of the cell rattled, the metal giving way and suddenly swinging open. She jumped into Drew's arms, moving away from the door.

"You need to leave. Now," a low baritone commanded, the figure unrecognizable in the dim light.

"Kristoff?" Drew said cautiously, tightening his arms around Talia. Maybe she wasn't terrified, but she wasn't stupid either. She'd moved like her ass was on fire the moment the door gave way.

The Sentinel king stepped into the dim light, his expression grim. "I'm sending you back to the human realm. Before you leave, I need you to give some information to Hunter," Kristoff demanded, his ice blue eyes shimmering in the darkened space.

Drew felt information transfer into his mind, sent to him by his king. "They're coordinates. What's there? And how can we leave here?"

"Hunter needs to find a…woman." Kristoff's voice tripped over the last word uncomfortably. "She'll explain when he's there. But it's imperative that he gets there. And I've arranged a trade with Goran for your release. I may not have been able to take Hunter's punishment in the human realm, but I can do a trade here."

A trade? What the hell would Kristoff trade to get them released?

"You're staying?" Drew couldn't think of any other way Goran would have agreed to release them. What was better than a Sentinel and a special *radiant*? There was only one thing better, more powerful, and it was having the king of the Sentinels as a willing prisoner.

Kristoff inclined his head slightly. "You and Zach are in charge during my absence."

"How long?" Drew asked impatiently. "How long are you going to be here in order to get us free?" He took Talia's hand and they left the cell to stand in front of Kristoff.

"I don't know," Kristoff replied gravely. "As long as it takes."

"We need you. You can't do this. Take Talia out of here and I'll stay if you need a casualty. Just get her to safety. The whole damn world is falling apart. You can't be a prisoner here." Drew's frustration was rising. No way in hell was he leaving his king to be slaughtered here.

"I don't die easily, Drew," Kristoff said with a slight smirk. "They can hurt me, but they can't kill me without difficulty. I can't say the same for you. Take Talia to safety and bind her to you. Once she's bound and her power is released, they won't pursue her. They want her because she has a very dangerous *radiant* ability that hasn't yet been released."

"What?" Drew asked desperately.

"I don't know for sure, but something bad enough for them that I almost couldn't get them to agree to a trade."

"Why trade at all?" Talia asked, her brow furrowing in concentration. "You're the king, and we're small comparatively."

"You're far from insignificant to the survival of mankind, Talia," Kristoff informed her. "You're the future of the Sentinels and of humans. Your power is essential in the righting of the balance of good and evil."

"Why?" she asked inquisitively. "And how do you know that?"

Kristoff's gaze softened as it landed directly on Talia. "Because you're my daughter."

"That's not possible." It took Drew a moment to even comprehend what Kristoff was saying, but when he did, he balked. "Sentinels don't have children unless they're mated. Are you saying that Talia's mother was your *radiant*?"

"Regretfully...no. I met her mother only once, but I was enchanted with her. I never knew that she was pregnant, and I didn't know I had a daughter until today. We're forbidden to have real relationships with humans, but I never forgot your mother, Talia. I wish I'd known you were my daughter." Kristoff's eyes shone with remorse as he looked at Talia. "I...learned that her pregnancy was foretold in the prophecies, but it was unrecognizable and vague. It was only discovered recently."

"H-how did you find out? And why did it happen at all?" Talia was visibly shaken, her fingers trembling as she nervously tucked a strand of hair behind her ears.

Drew looked from Kristoff to his woman, the emotion between the two of them almost palpable in the toxic air around them. Talia looked vulnerable, shaken, her emotions conflicted. Her thoughts were racing along with her emotions, the questions shooting through her mind like lightning. But underneath the logic, Drew could feel her longing for the father she'd never had.

Kristoff appeared remorseful and Drew could sense that his king's longing for his daughter was as great as Talia's.

"I told Drew your connection to a demigod was probably strong. It is. I was a demigod before I became the Sentinel king. Although I'm a Sentinel, I still retain my powers as a demigod. I still shouldn't have been able to father a child, but it was fated," Kristoff admitted, his eyes never leaving those of his daughter's. "I'm sorry, Talia. I don't regret that you exist. I only regret that I never knew."

"If you didn't know, then it isn't your fault," Talia told him reasonably. "My mother was never bitter. And she didn't hate you. She just never had much to tell me about you because she was only with you for one night. But I wondered." Talia fidgeted nervously. "Are you disappointed? I'm not beautiful like my mother, and I don't resemble you at all."

Drew had to hold back a growl. Talia was beautiful. She just didn't realize it.

"No," Kristoff said in a low, husky voice as he moved closer to Talia. "You're unique, wonderful, and smart. I'm proud to call you my daughter. When you started investigating the Sentinels, I started paying attention. I watched you, fascinated by the way your mind worked, by your intelligence. I was drawn to you for some reason, and I'm fairly certain that my close proximity was probably what set off your compulsions to research. When Drew mentioned them, I suspected that almost immediately. I assumed it was because I still had demigod blood and the way I watched over you so closely just kicked in your instincts. I didn't know you were my daughter, but I should have suspected something wasn't right. I felt the connection, but I never would have imagined we were related that way. I did know you were a special *radiant*, but I had no idea you were my child."

"You knew she was my *radiant*," Drew answered adamantly. "That's why you sent me after her."

"Let's just say I had a strong suspicion," Kristoff replied vaguely.

Strong suspicion, my ass. Drew knew that Kristoff had known exactly what he was doing when he'd sent Drew after Talia.

Drew watched as Kristoff placed a gentle kiss on the top of Talia's head. "You're my daughter." Kristoff's voice was rough with emotion. "There's nothing I wouldn't do to protect you now. Go back to the human realm with Drew. The future of the Sentinels and humans depends on you being there."

"What about you?" Talia asked tremulously, a lone tear rolling down her cheek. "We can't just leave you here. We can't. I just found you. I have so many questions—"

"Save them for later and I'll answer every one. Right now you must go," Kristoff said forlornly. Looking at Drew, he ordered, "Don't return. Do what you can about the chaos happening on Earth with the humans, but don't come back here. Both of you will be sick from the toxins here, but it won't be as severe as Zach's illness. Unlike Zach, you came here unwillingly, and the penalty for being here won't be severe. But don't come back. The Sentinels have no immunity and no powers here. Coming here would be suicide for them. Keep them safe. I expect you and Zach to obey my last command. And get Hunter to those coordinates."

Last command? "You are coming back, right? After the sentence is over?" Drew didn't like the sound of Kristoff's voice, the resignation he could hear in his king's tone.

"Until I return, I expect you and Zach to lead the Sentinels." Kristoff drew a ring from his finger, never completely answering Drew's question. "This is the ring that was bestowed on me when I became king. Wear it. The Sentinels will follow you."

"Why? You're coming back." Drew took the ring reluctantly.

"Until I do, I need you and Zach to assume leadership. This will allow you to rule in my absence," Kristoff said calmly. "Take care of my daughter," he added.

Talia broke her pensive silence with a small, plaintive cry, throwing herself into her father's arms. Kristoff's eyes closed as he held his daughter close for a moment, stroking her hair with one of his large hands.

"Come with us," Talia begged desperately. "The Evils have already broken the rules. Don't stay here. Please."

"I can't," Kristoff said gruffly. "The Evils may break the rules, but I'm Sentinel, and we are still bound by our honor and our vow. I can't leave here now." Kristoff opened his eyes and slowly moved Talia back to Drew's side.

As Talia's body disconnected from Kristoff's, something dropped out of the pocket of his leather jacket, landing silently on the dirt floor. She bent and picked it up, examining the scroll. "What's this?"

"Prophecies," Kristoff answered. "The demon prophecies. A bunch of gibberish that nobody really understands—even me."

"May I keep it?" Talia asked hesitantly. "I'd like to examine them."

"It's yours," Kristoff agreed, smiling fondly at Talia. "I already know them all by heart, even if I don't always understand them until after the fact. Make of them what you will." He slapped a hand to Drew's shoulder. "Stay safe and protect Talia."

Drew opened his mouth to reply, but in an instant, he and Talia were swept back to the human realm, leaving Kristoff behind.

Kristoff watched as Drew and Talia disappeared, his sense of relief greater than the dread of any punishment that awaited him. When he had made the agreement with Goran to let his daughter and Drew leave in return for his own imprisonment, he'd already known what his fate would be. Even if Talia hadn't been his daughter, he would have made the same deal. Drew and Talia were key to unlocking the mystery of how the Sentinels could once more reclaim balance with the Evils. Goran might think that he had gotten the better deal by taking the Sentinel king, but Kristoff knew he hadn't. His only regret was that he might never get to know his daughter. Chances were, he'd never see her again.

He blinked as he heard Goran's summons, the beckoning making him tear his eyes away from the spot where Talia and Drew had disappeared.

He'd made an unbreakable vow and he'd honor it.

Turning solemnly, Kristoff walked away, knowing it was time.

Chapter Ten

Talia arrived at Kristoff's home a mess, her limbs tangled with Drew's. But at least she was coherent. Her head was only spinning slightly, and she disentangled her legs from Drew's to lie next to him on the enormous bed that she had seen before she disappeared. She wondered if their landing site was a not-so-subtle hint from her father. "He's my father," she whispered reverently, propping herself up on one hand to look at Drew. "What will they do to him?" She was afraid she didn't really want the answer to that particular question, but she needed to know.

Drew looked up at her from his position flat on his back. "I don't know. I'm not certain what kind of bargain he made with them. We'll get him out of there somehow, Talia. I swear."

"Maybe the answer is in the prophecies," she wondered aloud, gripping the scroll her father had let her keep. "We can't leave him there."

"He isn't helpless, Talia. He's a damn demigod, a fact that he conveniently forgot to share with his friends," Drew told her, his voice sarcastic. "Why didn't he tell us?"

Talia could read the hurt underneath Drew's rancor. The fact that their king had been holding back information hurt him. "I'm certain he had his reasons," she assured him, running a soothing hand down his chest because she couldn't stop herself from touching him.

He caught her hand and entwined their fingers on top of his chest. "I can't believe he's your father. Are you feeling okay about that? It was a shock for me. I can only imagine how you feel."

"Well, other than the fact that he looks the same age as I do, and the other fact is that my father is a demigod and a demon, I guess I'm okay with it." She smiled at Drew tremulously. "Honestly, I don't know what to think. I'm worried about him."

"He'll be fine. We'll find a way to get him out of there." He raised their joined hands to his mouth and gave hers a gentle kiss before letting them fall back to his chest.

Talia's head started to pound, and her stomach began rolling. Putting the back of her hand to her forehead, she could tell she was burning up. "I'm not feeling so great." Her body felt like it was on fire, and the sudden onset of flu-like symptoms was unsettling. What the hell was happening to her?

"Toxins," Drew answered gravely. He cuddled her close to him and rested her head gently on his chest. "Sleep. Hopefully it won't last long."

"Are you sick?" she questioned, lifting her head to look at his face. She could tell he was feeling the symptoms, too.

His skin was damp and he was pale, but he answered, "No. I'm fine. Rest now."

Talia was consumed by exhaustion, her muscles screaming with pain. But the steady beat of Drew's heart underneath her ear calmed her, and finally lulled her into a deep, dreamless sleep.

The two of them lay like that until the next afternoon, entwined together in a healing slumber until they could function again.

Talia awoke disoriented and groggy, feeling as if she had a whopper of a hangover despite not having had a drop of alcohol that night before.

"It's daytime," she whispered under her breath, seeing the light seeping through the blinds of the window.

Everything that had happened rushed back into her mind in a heart-beat, and she sat up, searching for the scroll her father had given her, finding it next to her pillow. There was only an impression and tussled covers where Drew had slept. One glance at the clock beside the bed had her groaning and realizing that Drew was probably already awake. It was almost three o'clock in the afternoon.

A ball of fur launched itself onto the bed, brushing against Talia's arm. "Pumpkin," she cried happily, stroking her feline as the cat purred contentedly. "How did you get here?"

Continuing to purr loudly, Pumpkin looked at her like she'd asked a stupid question...which she had. How else would she have gotten here except Drew? "He brought you here, didn't he?" she asked Pumpkin thoughtfully. "And I'll bet he didn't use a cage." Drew "I-don't-like-cats" Winston was a fraud. He'd obviously thought about Pumpkin's welfare before she'd even had a chance to do it herself.

Moving gingerly to the side of the bed after she'd reunited with her cat, she got up and padded into the bathroom attached to the mon-strous bedroom. As she moved inside and closed the door, Talia turned around to find her own clothes and toiletries littering the countertop.

"Drew," she sighed softly, a little smile forming on her lips. The small gesture touched her heart as nothing ever had before. In addition to bringing her cat from his own home, he'd obviously fetched her things from her house and brought them here so she'd have them when she woke. What guy did that kind of thing? No man she'd ever known. Maybe she was just pathetic because those little things meant the world to her, but she knew Drew did it without thinking about it, as though it was his privilege and pleasure to take care of her. It was just one of the many things she loved about him.

I love him.

Talia wasn't just drawn to Drew by a mating instinct. She really did love him. Maybe she had tumbled into the state soon after she met him, or after admiring his strength of character that had helped him make it through the suffering he'd gone through during the Great Famine in Ireland. She could pick one of a million reasons to love Drew, but the truth was, she *did* love him. Maybe he was over-the-top protective, but she loved that, too. After being alone for so long, after feeling unloved for so long, the way that Drew cared about her was like an addictive drug. And being the subject of Drew's obsession was a habit she never wanted to kick.

He's under the mating influence. It doesn't mean he loves me.

Talia shook her head in denial as she quickly shed her clothing and stepped into the shower. He might not love her, but he cared. It was more than she had ever had from any other person in her life before, except her mom.

Feeling much improved after her shower, Talia stood in the hallway outside the bedroom, wondering exactly what it would take to win a piece of Drew's heart. She already had his soul. Was it really necessary to win his heart as well?

The pang in her chest told her that it probably was, and whether it was necessary or not, she wanted Drew's heart. She loved him enough to want the emotion returned to her. In fact, she craved it.

She looked up and down the hall with a small sigh, wondering which direction she needed to go. Dear old Dad had a gigantic house—a mansion—and she didn't have a clue where Drew was at the moment. She headed down the stairs, following the distant sound of male voices.

Zach and Drew were sitting at the table in the kitchen, both of them devouring plates of food. She walked over to the coffee pot, finding it still half full. Opening cupboard after cupboard searching for a mug, she felt a little guilty for invading Kristoff's things, but she was desperate for coffee.

"Good morning, beautiful." Drew's deep, sexy tones sounded behind her.

"It's afternoon," she reminded him, finding a mug and filling it with coffee. She wanted to tell him she wasn't beautiful, but she'd given up. Her entire body flushed with pleasure from the greeting, and she knew he didn't agree with her about her level of attractiveness, so she just enjoyed the feeling of an actual compliment.

"He's your father, you know. You have every right to drink his coffee," Drew remarked casually, his voice infused with humor. "How do you feel?"

She took a sip of her coffee. "Better. Are you okay?"

"As well as I can be, after spending the night together in bed with you just sleeping," he teased, his lilting accent making the words sound sexier and naughtier than they should have sounded.

Drew dropped his fork on his plate and fetched a plate from the oven. "I kept yours warm for you." He set it on the table with silverware and a napkin.

"You two cooked?" she asked, raising a brow at Drew.

Drew opened his mouth, but Zach answered, "I cooked."

"Which means he went and got food at a restaurant and we put your plate in the oven to keep it warm," Drew answered wickedly.

"Don't tell Kat," Zach said desperately. "I told her I was learning. I'm trying to be a supportive husband while she's going to school. But I have no talent for cooking. I get impatient and burn everything."

Talia sat, eyeing the extravagant breakfast in front of her. She looked at Zach, realizing he was completely serious. Okay…maybe there were a few other Sentinels who went out of their way to make their mates happy. Obviously poor Zach was trying desperately, but failing. "I think Kat probably already knows," Talia told him mischievously. She had no doubt Kat knew her husband didn't cook, but nevertheless loved Zach for trying. Talia doubted Kat gave a damn whether Zach could cook or not, but she had to love the fact that her husband tried because he wanted to please her. "If this is what you're giving her when she comes home from class, I have no doubt she knows you didn't go from kitchen disaster to master chef that quickly." Talia picked up her fork and dove into her food. She was hungry and hadn't eaten since her breakfast with Drew the day before.

Zach frowned. "You think she knows?"

Chewing her food, Talia nodded. She knew the one thing that irked the Sentinels is that they couldn't seem to produce decent food via magic.

"I'll try harder," Zach vowed. "What is that?" He was eyeing the scroll she'd set beside her plate.

Talia wanted to tell Zach that his wife valued his other qualities and wouldn't give a damn if he didn't cook. The man was a billionaire, and could afford to buy his food wherever he wanted. But she didn't bother. Talia was fairly certain Kat would set him straight soon enough. "They're demon prophecies. I want to study them."

Zach snorted. "Gibberish."

Drew nodded his agreement. "I caught Zach up on what happened. More and more humans are dying, and it's getting difficult to keep up with all the casualties so humans don't learn of our existence. And we need to get Kristoff out of the demon realm. If you want to study them, Talia, we'd be grateful. We're going to be busy trying to do what we can to lessen the damage going on right now."

Itching to look at the scrolls, Talia grabbed the prophecies and started to jump out of her chair. She never made it. Drew reached out and grasped her upper arm gently. "Finish your meal, Talia. A few more minutes won't matter. You haven't eaten since yesterday."

She glanced at Drew, sitting back down when she saw the stubborn look on his face. She wanted to tease him, tell him she could use to lose a few pounds, but she knew where that look was coming from, the look of a man who had seen so many people die during a famine. For Drew, eating wasn't a joking matter. "If I can figure out how the prophecies are worded or were revealed from those that have already happened, I might be able to decode what the others yet to come actually mean." She resumed eating, watching as the worried look on Drew's face started to soften.

Zach rose from his seat and his empty plate and utensils disappeared. Talia looked up at him, a bit startled.

Zach winked at her. "I may not be able to cook, but I do clean up after myself. I have to go. I need to go meet Kat." Zach looked at Drew. "We'll figure all this out. I'll be back later with Kat."

Drew nodded and Zach disappeared.

"Do you really think we can rescue Kristoff?" Talia asked anxiously.

"We have to figure out how we can get in and use our magic in the demon realm to help him. We also need to know what kind of deal he cut with the Evils to get us out. We can't take him out if it will kill him. He won't die easily because he's a demigod, but I don't like the thought of him suffering very long at the hands of those slimy little bastards." Drew looked at her, tormented. "But we'll figure things out. Zach and I are going to be busy trying to keep the Evils from revealing our presence on Earth. They aren't exactly being subtle anymore."

"Then Kat and I will work on a plan," Talia replied, dropping her fork to her empty plate and taking a sip of her coffee.

"You're my *radiant*, my mate," Drew protested.

Talia shrugged. "All the more reason for us to get involved. The Sentinels are in crisis, and my father that I've never even gotten to know is in the demon realm being held prisoner. Do you expect me to just sit back helplessly while you and Zach kill yourselves trying to save humankind? We may be female, but we're far from useless." She folded her arms in front of her and glared at him.

"It has nothing to do with you being useless. I don't want to see you hurt," Drew rumbled, bolting from his chair in frustration. "It's bad enough that I'll have to be away from you, leaving your protection to guardian Sentinels. I know Zach feels the same way about Kat."

"Get over it," Talia told him shortly, rising from her chair to stand in front of Drew. "You need help, and I'll do whatever I can. I want to be your partner. I don't have magical powers, but I have a brain."

"Believe me, I'm well aware of that. I have one, too, but it doesn't seem to function around you." His breathing was heavy, and he took a deep breath, letting it out before replying. "I want to be partners. I want you to be my mate forever. I want you to bind with me, Talia. Fuck! I *need* you to mate with me. I have to make sure you're mine right now. And safe."

Talia chewed on her lower lip, thinking. What the hell could she say to that? Drew was obsessed with her protection, and she knew it was a trait that was inbred because she was his *radiant* and because he was... well...Drew. Everything Sentinel inside him demanded he protect his mate.

"It's not just the demon in me," Drew said in a husky voice, his eyes glowing a light amber.

"What?" Talia questioned, knowing he'd picked up on her thoughts.

He moved forward and grabbed her by her upper arms, pulling her closer. "The man in me wants you protected, too. It's not just my mating instinct driving me, Talia. I want you out of harm's way."

Talia sighed. "But I'm not like most women, Drew. I sense evil. Or, at least, I generally do. I know I failed to recognize the Evils before they could take us to the demon realm, but I'm ready and aware of their ability to distract now—"

"And what about their next trick? Will you be ready for that? They're more powerful than before, Talia. Very little can protect you against them now." His nostrils flared and his expression was one of pure, male stubbornness mixed with carnal need.

"Then bind us together, Drew. There's never going to be anyone else for me except you." She reached up and stroked his hard jawline, her insides twisting with need. "I think I've been waiting for you." Maybe everything that had happened in her life had led up to this moment, this man. Nothing and no one else mattered at that moment. Only Drew.

"I need you to be sure, Talia. There won't be any going back after it's done. You can leave me, but I'll find you. Once we're bound together, I'll never let you go." His voice was rough and ragged, his gaze intense. "More than likely, I wouldn't be able to let you go now, but I can guarantee that once you're mine, nothing will keep me from you."

Drew was more fierce and feral than she'd ever seen him, but she wasn't afraid. In fact, every word he spoke did nothing but arouse her. This fiery, animalistic part of Drew actually beckoned her, made her body burn like blue flame. "I want to be yours. Take me as your mate." The fire he'd stoked in her wouldn't be denied. It went from her belly to her sensitive nipples and landed between her thighs, flooding her core with molten heat. "Please," she added softly, spearing her fingers through his hair and yanking his mouth toward hers, desperate to feel them connected.

"I plan on it," he whispered fiercely, demandingly, wickedly, his eyes now radiating golden flames. "And after that, you'll take me." His mouth descended, giving her no quarter, and swept her away in his dominant embrace.

Chapter Eleven

alia's whole body was quivering as she stood in front of Drew in the bedroom she'd just left a short time ago. Not that she was afraid of what was going to happen, but her whole being was trembling with the desire to be united with Drew. He'd transported them right after he'd thoroughly ravaged her mouth, and she hadn't even noticed until she opened her eyes to see his beloved face in front of her.

"You understand how the ceremony works?" Drew rasped, sounding like he was having a tough time holding himself together.

Yes. She knew. Drew had explained it during some of his revelations about the Sentinels and demon history. And she knew what was about to happen would be a hell of a lot more pleasurable for her than it was for him. Drew would be restrained, confined, and it would be difficult for him until she marked him. "Yes. Let's do it fast." She didn't want to draw out his torment any longer than she needed to.

Drew barked out a laugh. "So eager, are you?" he asked in a low, graveled baritone. "This won't be painful for me, *mo grha*. It will be a pleasure like no other. It will bind me to you." He slowly started to release the buttons on her shirt, his eyes never leaving hers.

"But the restraints—"

"Won't matter," Drew interrupted, placing a finger over her lips. "Being mated to you is something I want more than I've ever wanted anything in my entire existence. And doing it fast is not in the plan."

Drew finished with the buttons and slipped her shirt over her shoulders, letting it fall in a pool of silk to her feet. "What's the plan?" she asked softly, already shivering with arousal as the cool air hit her skin and Drew's palm stroked from the waistband of her jeans to her breasts. He traced each hard nipple through the silk of her bra. "I make sure you're ready for me."

Talia wanted to protest, to tell him she was beyond ready, but she only squeaked as Drew ripped the flimsy bra in half and her naked breasts spilled into his hands. He drew the tattered bra from her body impatiently and pushed her back against the large, wooden bedpost.

"Mine!" he declared possessively, his hands palming her breasts, teasing the nipples into agonizingly sensitive peaks. "You'll be ready to ride me, Talia. You'll want this mating as desperately as I do," Drew growled, one hand moving to the button of her jeans. His mouth licked and sucked each tender nipple, making her cry out in a sound that was both pleasure and pain. He placed her hands over her head, curling her fingers around the bedpost. "Hold on. Don't move," he commanded, his mouth barely taking a break from his assault on her breasts.

Talia gripped the post, actually glad for the support. "Please. Drew."

She watched as he dropped to his knees and grasped the waistband of her jeans, jerking down the zipper and yanking them over her hips. "Step out of them," he said abruptly.

Talia kicked out of the denim, and gripped the wood harder as Drew moved his hands up and down her bare thighs. Knowing she couldn't take much more teasing, she pleaded, "Please stop. I can't take anymore."

"You smell needy and intoxicating, Talia," Drew drawled, ignoring her plea and running his tongue over the outside of her saturated panties, tracing her folds with his tongue. "Do you know what it does to me knowing that only I can make you this way? That I can arouse you until the only thing you can think about is me fucking you until you come apart?"

Talia closed her eyes, leaning her head back against the post. She was needy. And downright desperate. "Then make me come before I lose my mind," she pleaded, both loving and hating Drew's dominance at the moment. Her pussy and clit were throbbing almost painfully, and as he stroked his tongue along the soaked material of her panties again, she let out an anguished moan.

Drew's control seemed to snap as he heard her sensual agony, and he ripped the lingerie from her hips with one firm, brutal tug. His hands curled over the back of her thighs, urging her legs farther apart and delving between her folds with so much aggression that it was nothing less than a claiming.

"Yes," Talia hissed, gasping as Drew's tongue sought and found her clit, rolling the bundle of nerves between his teeth and laving it with his tongue. Her hips thrust forward, begging for more. And Drew gave it to her. He feasted on her pussy possessively as his fingers moved up the inside of her thigh and sought her wetness. There was no hesitation as he thrust two fingers into her empty channel, filling it and claiming it completely. Her hips rocked forward again, her whole body igniting as he relentlessly thrust with his fingers and assaulted her clit with his tongue. An arm wrapped around her hips and his hand splayed over her ass, grasping it to hold her steady for the sensual assault he was lavishing on her.

Talia's head dropped down with a moan, her eyes focusing on the top of Drew's head, and she watched as he plundered her pussy with such unyielding, carnal, and erotic determination that just seeing him like that between her thighs was her undoing. She ripped her eyes away as pleasure rippled through her entire being, making her whole body shudder. "Oh, God." Talia wasn't sure she was going to live through this climax. It took her body over, and she had to grip the post to keep her legs from giving way beneath her.

Drew was unstoppable as she came, his mouth catching every drop of her liquid pleasure as if drawing nectar from her, prolonging her orgasm until it was almost too much.

He caught her as she fell, her grip on the bedpost weakening as her body pulsated violently. Scooping her up, he kissed her, his tongue thrusting into her mouth, her taste still on his lips. Wrapping her arms around his neck, she returned the pressure of his tongue, trying to tell him without words what this passionate encounter was doing to her.

His clothing disappeared as his marauding tongue continued to invade her mouth, leaving them skin-to-skin. He set her down on the bed, finally disengaging his mouth from hers.

Talia's gaze locked with his, fascinated by the spiraling amber fire in his eyes, which actually threw sparks of light into the air around them. "Drew," she murmured, still panting from the violence of her climax, entranced by the intensity of his stare.

"Now you're ready," he said arrogantly, but his expression revealed a tinge of vulnerability, too.

Talia's eyes moved over his ripped body: so perfect, and so damn masculine. "You're so beautiful," she whispered breathlessly, her fingers itching to touch the smooth skin over the steely bulk of his muscular build.

Drew crawled onto the bed to sit beside her. "I'm an Irish peasant, Talia. And part of me will always be an Irish peasant. I don't dwell on it, and I love being a Sentinel. But I've never forgotten where I came from. I'm far from pleasant to look at."

Talia frowned at him, wondering how he could find her beautiful, yet be totally unable to see his own allure. "Aside from being a panty-melting, gorgeous male, there are so many other things aside from physical appearance that make you beautiful to me," Talia argued, running her hand over his stubborn jaw.

Catching her hand, he pressed it to his mouth. "You're the only woman who I want to see me that way. So as long as you find me acceptable, that's all that matters. And your panties didn't melt—I tore them," he informed her, deadpan. "Take me now, Talia. I can't wait any longer."

Talia scooted over as Drew lay down on the bed, uttering a string of lyrical words that she didn't understand. His arms swept out to his sides and stopped, held immobile by invisible bindings. "Fuck! They really are unbreakable." The muscles in his arms and powerful legs strained, but his movement was limited. "Come ride me, Talia. I'll forget about them." His voice was demanding, authoritative even though he was the one restrained.

Talia watched him for a moment, eyeing the dominant male who put himself at her mercy just so she would be his, and it moved her more than she ever thought possible. The mating instinct overtook her as she saw him in that position, her instinct to claim him as her own undeniable. She longed to ride him until he was as overcome by desire as she was right now.

"Your need is nothing compared to mine," Drew groaned. "Fuck me, Talia."

The pain in his tone shook Talia out of her mesmerized trance and into action. He sounded tortured, and it squeezed at her heart. She eased onto his body, realizing he was throwing off heat like a furnace. Not hesitating, she moved over him, positioning his cock to her empty channel, needing him to fill her with an urgency that was soul deep. She took him in one forceful plunge, a stroke that filled her to capacity, and they groaned together as he sunk deep, the connection so sublime that Talia nearly climaxed again. Lowering herself over his body so they were skin-to-skin, she told him tremulously, "Tell me what you want, what you need. I'm not sure how to please you this way."

"You're already pleasing me, love. I'm exactly where I want to be." Drew lifted his hips as Talia bore down on him, burying himself even deeper than she could have imagined possible. "It arouses me even more knowing that you've never had a man this way. That it will only ever be with me," he growled possessively, his mouth taking hers as they moved together, Drew's urgency becoming ruthless.

Talia became submerged in a pleasure so intense that all she could feel was Drew and the volatility of their fierce and exquisite coupling. Their bodies moved as one, Drew burying his cock impossibly deeper with every downward movement she made, and having him fill her again and again, deeper and deeper, became her only thought, her only need. Her whole body was sensitized; the feel of Drew's moist skin sliding against hers was erotic, every emotion pounding at her raw and vivid.

Drew disconnected his mouth from hers with a violent twist of his head. "Mark me, Talia. For Christ's sake...do it now." His breath was hot and heavy against her neck, his voice commanding yet desperate.

Animalistic possessiveness flowed over her in waves, her need to mark Drew as hers as critical as breathing. Her teeth latched onto his shoulder, gripping his skin and muscle tightly with her teeth.

Mine! Drew is mine.

Her mouth released its grip, and she sat up, watching with deep satisfaction as the mating marked formed, even as Drew continued to bury his cock into her, pummeling upward so hard that she moaned. "Drew. You're finally mine. I love you so much." The words were out of her mouth before she could stop them, and really, she couldn't stop them, didn't want to stop them. Her emotions were on overload, every cell in her body energized from the vibrant connection she was experiencing with Drew. She was drowning in erotic pleasure, and she couldn't hold back the emotions pounding at her.

Talia was suddenly pulled from her hypnotic daze and she felt herself propelled through the air, landing on her back with Drew's massive bulk pressing her into the mattress. His look was ferocious and hungry as he snarled, "What did you say?"

"You're mine," she repeated.

He pinned her hands over her head, his cock still buried inside her, his body not moving. "Not that."

"I love you," Talia panted, her legs wrapping around his waist, urging him to start fucking her again. She needed it, and she needed it now.

"Say it again," he insisted. "Tell me again."

"I love you," she repeated, tears beginning to flow down her face. "Claim me, Drew. It hurts." It hurt that he didn't love her, too, but it also hurt to be unclaimed after she had already declared him as her own.

Drew moved his hands under her ass, pulled her hips up to his groin, joining them as closely as he could while he quickened the strokes of his cock.

"Mine. You'll always be mine," he said ferociously, his teeth clamping down on her shoulder, the mating mark starting to form almost instantaneously.

Talia was bombarded with a pleasure so intense that she started to climax immediately, her channel clamping down hard on Drew's cock as she experienced the most earth-shattering orgasm of her life. Her back arched beneath him, her entire body vibrating, Drew still holding her arms over her head in a dominating gesture. "I don't think I can take this," she screamed as she continued to climax violently and Drew's essence flowed into her, binding them together.

Drew groaned. "Mine." His body bucked as he released himself deep inside her, the internal wall muscles of her channel gloving his cock tightly, milking him.

Talia's heart was racing, and she was breathless as Drew rolled them over again, bringing her on top of him. He stroked her hair and ran a soothing hand down her back, cradling her like she was the most precious thing in the world to him.

"You are," Drew said gruffly. "There's nothing more important, not a person in the world I cherish more than you."

Talia marveled at her connection with Drew. Their thoughts and feelings flowed back and forth between each other like they were one instead of two. She could decipher which emotions were his and which were hers, but it was as though they had one soul, and everything they thought and felt belonged in that one place. It was like she was finally whole, but still herself. "Odd," she whispered, her heart still pounding against her chest wall.

"Incredible," Drew corrected. "I'd only ever heard of the connection between mates. It's not the same as feeling it."

Talia lifted her head, which seemed to take an enormous amount of effort since her body was limp and sated. "Does this mean you'll feel less protective? Now that we're officially mates?"

Drew laughed, a genuine sound of happiness that Talia had never heard from him before.

"You wish, *mo ghra*. I protect what's mine. I'm likely to be worse. But I'll try not to suffocate you with it." He shifted her to his side and cuddled her close. "Is it really so bad? Having someone worry about you?"

No. It wasn't bad at all. "I'm not used to it. I've always been alone, Drew. But no, it isn't bad. It's wonderful. It's only bad when you're being stubborn and unreasonable."

"Me?" he quipped innocently. "I'm never stubborn or unreasonable, love."

Talia snorted but she didn't comment. Drew Winston was the most stubborn individual, male or female, that she'd ever encountered, but it was one of the things she loved about him...most of the time, anyway. He was definitely tenacious.

"Tell me again, Talia," Drew demanded quietly.

She knew what he wanted to hear, but it was difficult for her to keep telling him that she loved him when he didn't love her in the same way. It stabbed at her heart, and if she kept saying it, it would be a scab that would never heal. Instead of speaking, she traced the lines of the mating mark on his shoulder, noting that it was exactly the same as the one she'd seen on Kat.

"Talia," Drew said huskily. "How can you think—"

"Drew!" Talia cried with alarm, feeling her body start to fade. "Something's happening." Her head began to swim and her image of Drew grew blurry.

"Talia! Hold on to me. Don't leave me." Drew grasped Talia more tightly, trying to hold onto her body, but within seconds he was clawing at thin air.

Drew tried not to panic, but he failed miserably. His breathing grew rapid and shallow as he scrambled out of the bed, bellowing her name. "Talia!"

Stay calm, man. Zach had freaked out and look how that turned out. All Drew could remember was that Kat had ended up in the demon realm after she and Zach had mated, unable to control her realm-walker powers that had emerged immediately after the two of them had mated. And Zach had definitely lost it when his mate had disappeared.

"Bloody hell!" Drew cursed, trying to remember what exactly had happened to Zach. "Kristoff reminded him that he was still connected to Kat," he rumbled, remembering how significant that had been.

Drew closed his eyes, his mind racing, trying to feel Talia's essence. They *were* connected now, joined by their souls.

He could feel her confusion, but he didn't sense that she was in pain or afraid. And she was close, in one single place, and not drifting from realm to realm. Her presence was solid, but that information still didn't keep him from feeling desperate to get to her.

Dressing himself with his magic, Drew closed his eyes and followed the trail of her spirit, knowing only that he had to find her. His demon might be demanding its mate, but Drew knew the man in him needed her more than his demon ever could.

His form dissolved, determined that he'd either find her, or die trying.

Chapter Twelve

Talia was mortified when she found herself transported to another room, in an unknown place that had the same décor as Kristoff's home, the same style, but God only knew where the hell she was.

She sat up slowly, pushing the hair from her eyes, realizing the humiliating fact that she was completely nude. "Shit," she cursed softly, looking around in a panic to see if she could cover herself.

"Problems?" a rough, low voice said from the other side of the room. "What are you doing in here?"

Talia's eyes shot to the other side of the room, only to find Hunter staring at her with an evil grin. He was lying on a massive bed, his head propped up by one arm, looking at her like women dropped into his bedroom every day. Did anything ever faze Hunter? "I'm naked," Talia said, stating the obvious as she drew her knees up to her chest to hide her body.

"I'd help you out, but I'm fresh out of powers," Hunter grumbled, swinging his feet over the edge of the bed and sauntering to his closet. Pulling out a robe from the back of the closet, he tossed it in her direction, keeping his eyes averted. "Use that. I sleep in the raw anyway. I hardly ever use it."

"Where am I? Am I still in Kristoff's house?" she asked Hunter nervously as she held the robe up to hide her nakedness.

"Technically, yes. This is the basement apartment," Hunter answered cautiously, as though he was still trying to figure out what the naked mate of another Sentinel was doing here.

Talia quickly wrapped herself in the black silk robe, pulling the sash closed with a hard jerk. She might be tall, but the Sentinels were massive, and it covered her from neck to toes. Scrambling to her feet, she had to reach for the arm of a chair to catch her balance. Her entire body was humming, a droning noise that kept getting stronger and stronger, louder and louder.

Her impulse to touch Hunter was confusing, and rather frightening. She tried to fight it, but she was drawn to him like a magnet. It wasn't the same way she was drawn to Drew, but more of an instinct, a magical compulsion to make contact with the Sentinel in front of her. "May I touch you, Hunter?"

Hunter just gaped at her, his expression incredulous.

Talia!

She could hear Drew's desperate bellow in mind, and she mentally called out to him, letting him know she was safe.

I'm with Hunter. I'm in the basement apartment. I'm fine, Drew.

"You want to touch me why?" Hunter rasped. "Nobody touches me unless they have to for penalties," he denied her.

Talia felt Hunter's pain more acutely than she ever had before, the aching loneliness that was nearly making him go insane. His rage was on the surface, but the real pain was deep inside him. "I don't know why. I just need to touch you. Please. It's painful." The droning was getting louder, her head beginning to spin.

"Fuck," he said irritably. "Then do it. Just don't do anything that will make Irish want to kick my ass or kill me."

Talia stepped forward cautiously, as though she were approaching a wild animal. Hunter wasn't completely broken. Because she was hurting, he'd agreed to whatever she needed him to do to help her. "It's not like that, Hunter. I don't know what it is, but it isn't sexual."

Hunter surprised her by holding his roughened palm out to her, and she placed her hand into his, the noise quickly quieting for her, but Hunter looked dumbstruck. Talia gripped his hand tightly, suddenly realizing exactly what was happening. "Your powers are returning to you." She could feel the transfer of an energy that wasn't her own flowing into Hunter's body.

Hunter's body shuddered as he momentarily gripped her hand tighter before finally releasing it. Shaking his head in denial, he said gruffly, "You mated with Drew?"

Lowering her hand back to her side, she replied, "Yes."

"And if you ever fucking touch her again, I'll kill you," Drew's angry voice informed Hunter from behind her. "What the hell are you doing?"

Talia spun around and put a palm on Drew's chest. "I asked permission from him to touch him. It wasn't his fault. Drew, this has to be my latent *radiant* power. I was drawn to Hunter because he was powerless. I'm obviously a conduit for lost powers of the Sentinels. I'm some kind of power restorer. Hunter's powers were bound. I'm clearly capable of releasing them or restoring them. They came to me, and I gave them back to Hunter. Why would the Sentinels need that kind of skill? How often do Sentinels lose their powers?"

Drew shot Hunter a still irritated look and asked, "Are they completely back?"

"Yeah. I can feel them," Hunter answered roughly.

"Sentinels don't lose their powers often in the human realm, but they're powerless in the demon realm." A third male voice entered the fray, and Talia saw Zach and Kat standing behind Drew. "Your power makes perfect sense," Zach muttered.

"Well, it doesn't make sense to me. Are you saying that Talia can be sucked into the demon realm at any time?" Drew questioned Zach, his eyes filled with rage.

"Doubtful," Zach answered calmly. "There are no Sentinels being held prisoner there except Kristoff, and he's under a bargain." Zach looked at Kat, and she nodded hesitantly. "I have something I need to tell you all."

"Spit it out," Drew growled. "I don't like the idea of Talia being vulnerable."

"When Kat and I were stuck in the demon realm, we saw human females there. For some reason, the Evils are keeping some women alive there. Human women. Kristoff said they're special, that they are able to recharge and not die when their souls are drained," Zach explained.

"*Radiants*," Kat and Talia said in harmony, smiling at each other as they spoke.

Talia shrugged. "It's the only thing that makes sense. Human females who recharge can only be Sentinel *radiants* who haven't yet lost their dormant power. The Evils pursued both Kat and I relentlessly. It's obvious they're after *radiants* who haven't yet mated. It's probably their source of increased power."

Zach and Drew looked at each other and slowly nodded. "Makes sense," Drew agreed aloud, pulling Talia closer to his side.

"Why is Kristoff in the demon realm?" Hunter asked hoarsely, his expression confused.

Drew quickly filled Hunter in on all that had occurred while he had been hiding away in his room, angry about the binding of his powers.

"Kristoff had a request for you. Are you going to do it? He said it was important," Drew asked, eyeing Hunter cautiously. "You can go slay demons now that you have your powers back, or you can honor the last request of your king."

Talia watched Hunter closely as rage flashed briefly in his eyes, and then turned to a look of stubborn determination. Obviously, Hunter's first instinct was to kill, but he had enough honor left to heed his king, even if said king had bound his powers.

"Kristoff pisses me off, but he saved my life. I'll see to it," Hunter agreed reluctantly.

Drew quickly gave Hunter the information Kristoff had given him. "There's a woman there Kristoff needs you to locate. I take it she's critical to helping us. That's all I gathered from Kristoff. His time with us was limited." Drew watched as Hunter nodded abruptly. "Our king traded his own life for mine and Talia's. I'd like to return the favor. I'm counting on you to find this woman, Hunter. If this woman can help, we need her."

"Kristoff is my father, Hunter. Please do this for him, and for me," Talia begged. "I know it shouldn't have happened, but it did. He got my mother pregnant, and I'm his daughter. He's the father I never got to really know. If we can save him, I want to give that possibility every chance." Talia reached out and touched Hunter's arm lightly in a silent plea, ignoring the low, growling noise she heard rising in Drew's throat.

Hunter looked startled at Talia's revelation, but he didn't ask any questions. He simply inclined his head again and disappeared without a word.

"Were you doing that to distract him, to keep him from beheading more Evils?" Zach asked Drew curiously.

"No. It actually was Kristoff's request. Whoever this woman is, Kristoff thinks she can help Hunter." Drew's voice was grave, but slightly hopeful.

"I sure the hell hope so," Zach answered quietly. "He might be a pain in the ass, but we've been brothers for a long time. I want the asshole alive and safe."

Drew was hurting over Hunter. Talia could feel his pain as surely as she could feel her own. The gradual decline in Hunter's sanity troubled him deeply, and she was willing to bet that it did the same to Zach. Although they were both covering up their anguish over their brother with a "tough guy" mentality, Talia knew they cared about him more than they could express.

"I can't believe Kristoff is your father," Kat said, shaking her head.

"He is. Pretty amazing, I know," Talia agreed.

"How?" Kat asked curiously.

"Brother, if your mate doesn't know how that happened by now, you aren't doing your job very well," Drew teased Zach, his voice amused.

Zach flipped Drew the middle finger and grasped Kat around the waist. "I've taught my wife plenty, and it would take me an eternity to show her everything I know," Zach boasted arrogantly.

Talia looked at Kat and they both rolled their eyes. "If this is going to be a caveman competition, I'm leaving. I have scrolls to study," Talia told Drew, pulling away from him.

"You have scrolls?" Kat asked excitedly. "Which ones?"

"The demon prophecies," Talia told her enthusiastically. "Kristoff gave them to me."

Kat squealed. "I want to have a look, too." She rushed over to Talia and grabbed her hand, ready to pull her from the room.

"Wait," Drew demanded. "Zach and I have business to attend to. Humans are being slaughtered, and we need to check on the warrior Sentinels and see what's happening. But I have one thing I have to do first."

Talia looked at him questioningly. "What?"

He looked at her intensely, and Talia gasped as the robe she was wearing was replaced by her own clothing, a V-neck shirt and jeans. "The robe smelled like Hunter. I don't like the smell of any other male on my woman. If anything happens, call out to us. You'll be watched over by the guardians until we return."

"Yes, master," Talia snapped back at him, more than a little irked by his arrogance.

Drew smirked at her, and Talia could feel his amusement underneath his alpha exterior.

I think that particular game is a little advanced for you, mo chridhe. But we can try it if you like. Problem is, if I had you at my mercy, pain would be the last thing on my mind.

Talia's irritation drained away, replaced by a rosy flush that covered her entire body as she heard Drew's sexy, naughty words in her mind. Suddenly, the idea of being completely under his control was one of the hottest thoughts imaginable.

Maybe I don't want to play. Talia tilted her chin and her eyes met his, her body melting as she saw the glint of amber in his eyes.

Then it will be my mission to convince you. His accent made the low, hot statement sound almost like a deep, throaty purr. *Stay safe, love.*

Any anger Talia had was gone, replaced by her concern for Drew, and the events that were currently taking place with the Evils. *Be careful. Please.*

Drew nodded slowly. *I intend to. I have you to come home to now.*

Talia watched as Drew and Zach vanished, her gut clenching from not knowing what the two of them were up against and what would happen.

Kat squeezed her hand. "I know how you feel. It's scary out there right now."

"I love him," Talia admitted simply, following Kat as she headed toward the bedroom door.

"Of course you do," Kat answered with a laugh. "He's a Winston. They're hard to resist." Kate dropped her hand and walked out the door ahead of Talia.

Talia followed, knowing Kat was right. But Drew was *her* Winston, and even knowing how capable Drew was, it didn't stop her from worrying any less.

Two days later, Talia and Kat were sitting at the kitchen table, still trying to decipher the prophecies. Drew and Zach hadn't been back since the day they'd disappeared from Hunter's room, and the two women were working frantically to help by figuring out the words on the scrolls.

Talia touched her mind to Drew's often, but he was blocking almost everything from her, only leaving a pathway open so he could hear if she called. She knew he was exhausted and frustrated, but when he spoke to her in her mind, he didn't mention any of those things. He reassured her he was fine, and nothing more. Zach did the same with Kat, but neither woman was fooled. Zach and Drew were facing some pretty tough odds.

The guardians were non-intrusive, but Talia could feel their presence constantly. And she knew there were more than just one or two. Honestly, she wouldn't be surprised if Zach and Drew had them surrounded by a whole fleet of guardians.

Kat had decided to take some time off from her classes, her mind too focused on the Sentinel crisis to think about her studies. The two of them had spent almost every waking moment trying to figure out what was still to come in the future of Sentinels versus Evils.

So far, Talia had been able to identify previous events because she knew what had already happened, and she thought she was getting closer to being able to decipher the future using the phrases that had been used before.

"Look at this." Talia pointed her finger at a particular passage, turning it around so Kat could see. The prophecies had been translated to the English language, which might account for some of the meaning being lost in translation.

The majesty of the Sentinels will fall, but will rise again if the light can be seen in the darkness.

Talia read the sentence aloud thoughtfully, watching Kat wrinkle her brow in concentration.

"In some of the other passages, majesty stood for king rather than the obvious meaning. I think this refers to Kristoff. And the light is a *radiant*." Talia's gut instinct told her she was right. "And Hunter is referred to as well." She pointed to another line for Kat to look at.

When rage meets power, rage will be calmed by the untried creator, and divinity will once again be free in a different form, if divinity and anger can exist together.

"Power, creator, and divinity have both stood for a god or goddess in previous passages. I think the rage is Hunter. I'm a little shaky on the rest of the prediction. Is it possible that Hunter is going after a goddess who still exists?" Talia once again got a pang in her gut, a certainty that some of what she was decoding was true. "Kristoff said that the Sentinels were more bound to their rules than the Evils. The only way that could really be true is if their source and creator were still on Earth. The gods who created the Evils are gone. But what my father said could be true if I'm right. If the god or goddess who helped create the Sentinels still exists, it binds them more tightly to their honor and pledge they made to the creating deity."

Kat looked up at Talia and smiled. "The way you think scares me sometimes. But I have a feeling you're right. It all makes sense, in a weird sort of way."

"After reading the prophecies, I think you and I are part of a bigger plan. Think about it, Kat. You can enter different realms. I can return power to the Sentinels. We really can enter the demon realm and rescue those women and my father."

Kat raised a brow and took a large sip from a mug of coffee. "Zach will let me into the demon realm again when Hell freezes over. He was ready to go alone before Kristoff made him realize it was suicidal, but he won't even talk about the fact that I can get them into that realm."

Talia had a feeling Kat was right, and Drew would have the same reaction, but... "It may become critical that we do get in. It already is for the sake of my father and those women. But we need something more."

"I've always known the day will come when I'd need my powers for entering the demon realm. Zach won't like it, but when we can get in and out to rescue Kristoff and the women, I'm doing it," Kate told her adamantly. "Kristoff taught me enough to control the powers, and I get better with them every day. And now that you can restore power to the Sentinels after they get in, we're closer than we've ever been. I can't stand the thought of those women suffering, and with Kristoff there, too, we have to find a way."

"It's not just the rescue. The balance between good and evil needs to be restored, Kat. The future of the Earth depends on it. The future of the Sentinels, too."

"What else do you think we need?" Kat asked curiously.

"Firepower," Talia replied. "The Evils have more power than the Sentinels do, and they have very few rules, now. The Sentinels need more power or they'll never be able to achieve the balance."

"Hunter?" Kat guessed. "Do you think whatever mission Kristoff sent him on is to obtain what we need?"

"I think so. I'm hoping it's what we need to drive back the Evils. Even if Drew and Zach can calm the situation right now, it won't last." Talia hated to voice the words that she knew were true. She wanted to believe the Sentinels could drive the Evils back to their own realm, crying for their mommies. But the truth was, the balance of might was uneven. The only advantage the Sentinels had was their intelligence.

Kat released a long sigh. "Waiting is hell."

Talia couldn't have agreed more.

Pumpkin jumped into her lap, whining woefully. As Talia stroked her fur, she couldn't help but wonder if her cat was crying for Drew. If so, she knew exactly how she felt.

Chapter Thirteen

rew returned the next day, looking wearier than Talia had ever seen him. His entire body was littered with lacerations and bruises. He'd obviously cleaned himself up, but it was hard to miss the fact that he was beaten all to hell.

He'd told her the Evils had been driven back to the demon realm for now, the warrior Sentinels taking a lot of casualties to accomplish that mission. Talia had been able to see the sorrow of the loss of every Sentinel on Drew's face.

Zach had taken Kat home, and Talia had climbed into bed with Drew. He'd been asleep almost from the moment his head hit the pillow.

She'd risen the next morning, trying to shower and dress as quietly as possible so Drew could catch up on his rest.

She went downstairs to cook, determined to feed Drew the moment he woke up. She'd caught up on her own research projects for work during the last few days, completing one of the texts that was coming due very shortly, and that had been neglected during her mystical compulsion to research demon history. As she prepared a massive breakfast, she wondered about the fact that she didn't miss her home in Idaho at all. For years it had been her sanctuary, but also her prison, her place to hide away from the world and the people in it. Now, she wondered how she had managed to live in that kind of isolation.

Because it's all I knew.

But over a short period of time, Drew had changed all of that, bringing her into a world where she actually had friends...and family. Maybe her weirdness really wasn't weirdness at all. Maybe she was just...different from the norm. But here...she fit.

What are you doing, love?

She'd felt Drew stirring before he actually spoke to her telepathically. She pictured him tousled and naked in bed, his massive body stretching before he tumbled out of bed.

Cooking. She answered him with a smile, flipping the pancakes over with a practiced flick of her wrist.

I'll be right there. His tone was hopeful.

Talia's chest ached, and she whipped up the rest of the breakfast with double portions, knowing Drew could eat the majority of it. She doubted that her desire to feed him would ever go away, and that his desire to eat would ever subside. She actually hoped he always ate this way, enjoying everything he had access to now after nearly dying of starvation.

"I'm more hungry for you than I am for food." Drew's arm snaked around her waist, pulling her back against his rock-hard body. "I woke up and you were gone. The only thing next to me warm and purring was the cat."

Talia smiled. "She loves you. And don't try to tell me you didn't talk to her this morning or give her a morning dose of affection." Pumpkin had jumped up into Talia's place the moment she'd gotten out of bed, curling up beside Drew like she owned him.

"I don't like cats," Drew replied with very little conviction behind the declaration.

Pumpkin strolled into the kitchen behind Drew, rubbing against his leg affectionately. Talia turned and lifted a brow at him. "Really?"

"Bloody hell! She's still a menace," he said unhappily, reaching down to pick up the plump cat. He went to the cupboard and opened a can of tuna and set it on the floor, letting Pumpkin down to devour it from the can.

Talia put her hands on her hips, biting her lower lip to keep from laughing. "She can eat cat food, you know."

"She's particular," Drew answered defensively.

"Because you're spoiling her," Talia replied with a laugh, unable to hold it back.

"Nothing wrong with eating well," Drew grumbled, watching as Pumpkin devoured her fish. "Food is important." Turning away from the cat, Drew slipped behind her, his arms once again encircling her. "I'm hungry," he reminded her, stroking his hands over her abdomen.

Talia shivered as his hot breath hit the sensitive flesh of her ear, his low, husky baritone making her panties damp and her face flush. "I've never cooked for you before. Sit."

"I missed you, *mo grha.*" He didn't let go. He drew her closer, turning her so he could kiss her.

His words tugged at her heart, and her arms slipped around his neck, marveling that this incredible man was actually hers.

Drew pulled her away from the hot stove before he devoured her lips and mouth with his, staking his claim on her, body and soul, with one scorching hot kiss. Talia melted against him, relieved that he had come back to her in one piece.

I missed you, too. The thought flowed from her to him easily as he took his time tasting her, claiming her.

Finally, Talia ended the kiss, worried her breakfast was going to burn. "Sit," she asked again, her voice a little less firm than it had been before. For her, Drew was the ultimate temptation, and she was doubtful there would ever be a time when she didn't want him. "Tell me what happened."

Drew demolished his breakfast, telling her about the battle with the Evils as he plowed through his eggs, bacon, sausage, and pancakes. Talia sat, slowly eating her own plate of food and drinking her coffee as they talked.

Finally, when he had finished catching her up on the last few days, she told him about her theories. "I think whatever Hunter is doing is important. It's in the prophecies."

"It makes sense. But what god or goddess could still be alive?" Drew said, frowning.

"I'm not sure. I don't know if my father was just saying it was a female to throw us off track, or if it really is a goddess. But I know it's important. It has to be one of the final pieces to the puzzle of how to rescue those women and my father."

Drew glanced up at her, sending her an obstinate look. "Tell me you don't plan on being part of this rescue plan," he stated dangerously.

"You have to know that Kat and I are part of what's happening right now, Drew. There's a reason we have these abilities."

"No," he stated ominously, his stormy gaze meeting hers. "Not happening."

Talia took in a breath and let it out slowly. Sometimes guys could be so short-sighted. "So you'd rather I live in a world full of Evils where no place is safe? What if we have a child someday? I know it's rare, but it could happen. Do you want our baby to live in a dark world filled with evil?"

Drew's eyes started to shoot fire as he looked at her. "Bloody hell! I want to take you someplace where no one will ever touch you, ever threaten you. Everything inside me tells me to hide you away in some remote place so the Evils can never touch you," he rasped, his breathing labored.

"And what if no place on Earth is safe? Then what?" Odds were, if the Evils tipped the balance too far, that kind of world would be a reality. Talia knew how hard this was for Drew, that his demon side ruled sometimes, but he had to understand that some things were worth fighting for, no matter what the risks.

"Controlling the Evils is worth almost any risk except losing you," Drew said huskily, rising from his chair and moving around the table to pull her from her seat. "Or any child we may or may not have some-day." He pulled her roughly against him, his arms coming around her like steel bands. "Ask me for anything, but don't ask me to willingly put you in danger. I can't." Drew's tone was angry and desperate at the same time.

"I love you, Drew. More than anything or anyone else in the world. But I'm going to ask some day. And I hope you'll rethink your answer. If I'm part of the prophecies, it has to be done." Talia sighed and laid her head against his shoulder, twining her arms around his neck. Maybe by the time she and Kat needed to act, Drew would love her, accept her for what and who she was, and respect what she had to do.

"Do you honestly believe I don't love you already? That I didn't fall hard and fast almost from the very beginning?" Drew moved, pushing her backward and against the kitchen wall. "Look at me, Talia."

Damn. The connection of their minds made it almost impossible for him not to discern her thoughts. "You've never said," she answered, focusing her eyes in the middle of his chest, remembering her murmuring the truth in a moment of passion, and not hearing it back from him.

He gripped her chin, forcing her gaze to his. "I never had a chance, since you disappeared before I could say the words." His voice was graveled, his stare incredibly stormy and intense. "What's it going to take to convince you, so I'll never again feel or hear your doubt?"

Talia had doubted her lovability all of her life, so she had no idea when she'd actually accept it. "Maybe when you tell me," she teased lightly, her heart begging him to say the words, and her body wanting his to show her.

Drew crowded her, trapping her between his muscular body and the hard kitchen wall. "I love you," he said in a low, guttural voice as he leaned down to nuzzle her ear. "I love everything about you, *mo grha*. I even love your stubbornness, even though it's likely to make me crazy," he continued, raining kisses over her face and neck.

Talia speared her fingers in Drew's hair, her heart thundering wildly against her chest wall. Red-hot licks of flame rose wherever he touched, suffusing her whole body. She fisted his hair as he tasted the sensitive flesh at her neck, her body already crying out for her mate. "Drew, I need—"

"I love you," he said again, tearing open her shirt with one tug, sending the buttons up the front scattering all over the kitchen floor. He moved his leg between her thighs, letting her straddle it.

Talia moved shamelessly, letting her heated, liquid core slide along his muscular leg, cursing the denim that was in her way. "Inside me," she begged, needing more.

"I love you," Drew said once again, his fingers teasing her nipples through the light, lacy fabric that barely covered them. "And I'm going to tell you again while I watch you come for me."

Talia moaned, needing more of Drew between her thighs than just this, although her hips rotated wildly against the rock-hard muscles of his leg, her body straining for a release that was being denied to her.

"I'd never deny you that, Talia. I just want to make it sweeter," Drew told her gruffly, reaching down to release the button and zipper of her jeans.

Talia wanted to tell him it was already going to be sweet, but her breath caught in her lungs as Drew's fingers slowly slid into her panties, meeting nothing but damp passion and heat.

"Christ. I love the way your body responds to me," he muttered harshly against her neck.

"I can't help it," Talia told him with utter abandon. "The moment you touch me, I need you inside me."

"I don't want you to be able to help it. I want to feel you and watch you come apart for me," he said demandingly.

He was getting what he wished. Talia was nearly insane with need, whimpering as one of his fingers slowly traced over her clit, ramping up her need for him until she couldn't form a single coherent thought. "Fuck me, Drew. Please."

He grasped the back of her head, tilting it upward with a gentle tug on her hair. Talia saw a quick glimpse of his fire-like eyes before his mouth came down on hers in a powerful embrace that rocked her to her soul. He claimed her mouth, invading her with his heated tongue: exploring, possessing, devouring, and adoring all at the same time. Opening to him, she accepted all he wanted to give her, pushing her tongue back against his with a needy moan, showing him how much she wanted him.

Come for me, Talia.

Drew spoke to her in her mind, removing his leg from between her thighs as his hands moved to cup her ass. She gasped into his mouth as he impaled her, pressing her back hard against the wall as he buried his cock to the hilt inside her, having dealt with the encumbrance of their clothing with a mental command. At that moment, their minds and souls intermingled, their bodies connected; they were one. They had the same needs, the same wants, and they strained as one to reach the pinnacle together, each pummeling stroke of Drew's cock lifting them both higher and higher. She pulled her mouth from his to take a breath, her heart racing and her breathing ragged as Drew pounded into her relentlessly, unceasingly.

"Mine," Drew huffed possessively, gripping the cheeks of her ass tighter.

Talia's arms were still around Drew's neck and as she spotted the mating mark, *her* mating mark, on his shoulder, she moved her head forward, put her mouth over it, and nipped at it, as though it would make him more hers than he already was.

Drew growled, as though her actions had just inflamed him even more.

Her climax was swift and merciless, slamming into her body in pulsation after pulsation. "Yes," Talia screamed, the back of her head hitting the wall behind her. Her body rocked against Drew's as he groaned, "I love you, Talia. Only you. I love you so fucking much it scares me."

His big body shuddered as his scalding release flooded her womb, his fiery stare consuming her as he watched her tremble with her own orgasm, letting herself go completely, trusting Drew to hold her to the earth as she shattered.

They clung to each other, breathless. Talia wanted to drop her legs to the ground, but thought better of it, not sure if her shaky limbs would hold her.

Two seconds later, they were both dressed and Drew swung her up into his arms as though she weighed nothing, his legs eating up the distance to a recliner in the living room. He sat, bringing her down on top of him, holding her against his body, his heart hammering beneath her ear.

"I love you," he stated again, his tone a little stubborn this time. "So don't ask me to throw you into harm's way. There's little I wouldn't do for you, *mo grha*, but that's one thing I can't do."

Talia peeked up at him to find his eyes gleaming with a warning not to argue. "Is it you, or your demon?" Somehow she was going to have to find a way to tame whatever was causing him to be so protective. Just a little.

"Both. It might be easier if it were one or the other, but every part of me wants you safeguarded," he answered gruffly.

Talia sighed. She'd figure it out in time. Everything was so new for both the man and the demon holding her so covetously. Hopefully one of them would lighten up, because the time was coming for some of the prophecies to be fulfilled, and she couldn't let them *not* happen. Too much depended on her and Kat doing what they were born to do.

Drew was her heart and soul. And she understood his reluctance to see her in a dangerous situation. Hadn't she felt the same way when he'd had to go off to fight the Evils, push them back into the demon realm? It had been all she could manage not to throw herself at him and make him stay.

"Things aren't always the way we want them to be," Talia answered quietly.

"Tell me about it. If I had my way, we'd be married and on a very long honeymoon right now. I'd show you all the places you've only studied in books," Drew answered unhappily. "After we finally got out of bed," he added, his voice a little lighter.

Talia's heart skipped a beat, her spirit soaring that Drew knew exactly what she'd always wanted. She did want to travel, see some of the places she'd never been able to see. It really hit her then that all Drew really wanted was to make her happy, see her be safe and healthy. "I love you. And we can do all those things when all of this is over." She kissed him softly on the lips. "Is that one of the perks to being married to a billionaire demon?" she teased him softly.

"One of many," he told her, raising a mischievous brow.

Talia reached over and snatched one of Drew's favorite truffles from the coffee table and unwrapped it, holding it up to his mouth as she said, "And then there are these little chocolate menaces. I think I've become addicted to them," she told him with a sigh.

Drew reached up and took the candy from her hand and bit into it, chewing slowly as he held the other half up to her mouth. "Share with me?" he rumbled, his eyes telling her that he was talking about more than food.

Even though she'd eaten a ton of them while Drew had been gone, she took it anyway, licking the chocolate from his fingers slowly. "Delicious," she declared cheekily. "And I'll always share with you."

Drew's eyes grew dark, and Talia visualized an image in her mind of her licking chocolate from another part of his body, a scene that was drifting through Drew's head. In the vision, his head was thrown back, his hands fisting her hair as she took his cock into her mouth, sucking chocolate from him as she moaned around him, naked.

"Drew!" Talia flushed and smacked him on the shoulder. "Do you ever stop thinking about sex?" Really, she was probably a hypocrite, because that steamy scene had dampened her panties. There was nothing she'd love more than to make Drew come apart like he did to her.

He gave her a wicked, wicked grin. "Nope. I used to be obsessed with food. Now I'm obsessed with you. If some kind of food is involved, all the better."

"But you weren't…"

"Eating?" he finished for her. "I could be."

Another naughty image flowed through her head, with her being featured as Drew's erotic feast. Talia squirmed in his lap, her body responding to his carnal thoughts. "Stop. We just had crazy good sex against the kitchen wall."

"Never tease a demon, *mo stór*. We're insatiable with our mates," he cautioned with a smirk.

Talia felt the proof of his statement under the cheeks of her ass. Drew was rock-hard…again. "Prove it," she challenged. "I'd like to try out those fantasies of yours."

"You'll be sore, love," he told her regretfully.

"Not if I'm on my knees," she answered in a sultry voice, her mind full of images of the things she wanted to do with Drew.

Drew gulped, his throat visibly contracting as he swallowed. "*That's* the fantasy you want to try out?" he croaked. "I was just teasing."

"I'm not," she told him, palming his erection under her ass. She grabbed a handful of truffles, gesturing to them. "I assume you can melt these for me."

He nodded, his eyes hooded.

"Take me to the bedroom, Drew. I'm suddenly feeling very hungry."

Talia loved the hot and fierce look in his eyes as he stood with her still in his arms. She could get to him. This incredible, scorching alpha male made her feel like she could fly if she wanted to.

He took the stairs two at a time.

And he definitely melted the chocolate, along with melting her heart once again.

Epilogue

alia and Drew were married the very next day, with Kat and Zach standing as witnesses at the county courthouse.

Talia didn't mind. In fact, she'd asked for it to be that way. With her father incarcerated in the demon realm, with Hunter's whereabouts still unknown, and with the uncertainties of what the prophecies foretold, not to mention what fate had in store for the world, she didn't want a lot of fanfare. And, more to the point, she didn't want to waste another moment not belonging to the man she loved. She *needed* to belong to Drew, and *needed* him to belong to her.

They celebrated at Drew's home with a small dinner party with food from one of the finest gourmet restaurants in the area. And, of course, a cake. And fresh salmon as a special celebration treat for Pumpkin, Talia's cat-Cupid extraordinaire, who had brought Talia and Drew together in the first place.

Talia and Kat had gotten a little tipsy on the champagne, while Zach and Drew remained perfectly sober, a characteristic of all Sentinels. Alcohol didn't intoxicate them.

Kat had dragged Talia outside for a breath of fresh air, saying they both needed a little breather after a few glasses of champagne.

Talia sighed as she stared at the beautiful diamond ring on her finger, holding it up to the light to watch it sparkle. "I can't believe I'm married. I didn't think that would ever happen. Sometimes I still think I'm dreaming."

Kat took a sip of the bottled water she'd taken outside with her, giving Talia a puzzled look. "Why?"

"I'm not exactly a guy magnet, Kat. And Drew is just so incredible. It's hard to believe he's mine."

"I know what you mean," Kat replied dreamily. "It's been a little while for me and Zach, but I sometimes still find it hard to believe that he finds me that irresistible." She smiled at Talia. "Are you happy?"

Talia wasn't sure "happy" could really explain how she felt, but she answered, "Yes."

Before Drew, her life had been empty, lonely. And it likely would have stayed that way had he not come into her life. "Sometimes I feel like the ugly duckling who's suddenly a swan."

"Sentinels are raw. They see only with their souls and then with their hearts with their *radiants*," Kat answered with a sigh.

"Thank God!" The two women spoke emphatically together, turning to look at each other and laughing out loud.

Talia looked up at the stars, dazzled by the tiny flecks of light. "I wish Kristoff could have been here. And I'm worried about Hunter."

"Me too," Kat admitted. "Hunter should have checked in by now. He's capable of flashing back and forth in an instant. Unless something happened."

Drew and Zach opened the sliding door, stepping out into the night with their women. "We got lonely," Drew admitted, wrapping his arms around Talia's waist.

She leaned back against him, for the first time in her life feeling complete.

Zach held his wife in the same manner, a comfortable silence between all of them as they all looked up into the night sky.

I love you , Drew told her in her mind. *I might not deserve you, but I'll cherish you every day for eternity.*

Talia's eyes watered with her overwhelming emotions as she covered Drew's hands around her waist with her own, savoring their connection. Kat was right. The Sentinels *were* raw, and she was grateful for it.

Drew loved her exactly as she was, and even felt unworthy of her love. But she'd work every day to make the stubborn Irishman realize that his love was the most precious thing in her life, and always would be.

I love you, too. She sent the emotion and words back to him, and let out a long sigh.

There were challenges ahead for the Sentinels, but she intended to make sure that she and Drew faced them together.

"Happy?" Drew whispered aloud in a husky voice.

Talia turned in his arms, seeing a slight look of apprehension on his face. Was he really worried that she'd regret being mated to him? "Ecstatic," she replied, wrapping her arms around his neck and proceeding to show him just how elated she was, by pulling his head down to hers and laying the sexiest kiss she could manage on his mouth.

Zach and Kat disappeared silently, leaving Talia alone with Drew, and she spent the rest of the night showing her new husband just how crazy she was about him, and how very much she loved him, even if he was a stubborn demon.

Hunter Winston had never been a pleasant man, even on a good day. And today wasn't even remotely close to one of those good days.

Even when he was human, he'd been a bastard, a man more concerned with his own pleasures than anything else in his life. And as a Sentinel, he hadn't changed a bit.

"Fuck!" He wasn't sure what the hell was guarding this woman he was seeking, but it seemed like he took one step forward and two steps back, never getting any closer to the coordinates Zach had given him.

He'd rather be lopping off the heads of Evils right now, but he still had a thread of honor left—albeit deeply buried—a part of him that owed a debt to Kristoff for saving his life. Sometimes, he wasn't sure if being spared had actually been a blessing or some sort of Hell that he'd been living in for well over a hundred years.

He kept moving, feeling like he'd landed in some sort of enchanted land: the kind with flesh-eating plants, carnivorous beasts, and other assorted obstacles meant to keep everything and everyone out.

He couldn't transport, which really pissed him off. He'd gotten his powers back, only to lose them in this shithole of an area again.

Was he in another realm? Or was this area really enchanted? He didn't have a goddamn clue. He knew he wasn't in the human realm in Washington—at least, not the normal Washington—and he wanted to get the hell out of here worse than he'd wanted anything in his life, other than to slay Evils.

Kill. Kill. Kill.

The impulse to annihilate Evils was pounding at him relentlessly, and he was losing his will to keep up this senseless trek.

He swatted at another plant, feeling more as if he were in the jungle rather than an unpopulated area of the Olympic Peninsula. If he had a little dog named Toto, he'd be telling it that they weren't in Washington anymore. Problem was, he wasn't Dorothy, he didn't have ruby shoes, and he couldn't give a shit if he got home anymore.

All he wanted, all he needed, was to slay Evils until the pounding in his head went away.

Kill. Kill. Kill.

But the vision of Talia's pleading look, and the debt he owed Kristoff made him keep moving forward, every step he took getting heavier. He was like a human again, most of his powers gone, and he was beaten all to hell from the days he'd spent trying to claw through the hazardous environment.

"Who the hell is this woman, anyway?" he growled, flinching as a tiny bird with razor-sharp teeth took a hunk of skin off his face. Followed by another, and then another.

He swatted them away and ran a hand down his face, cursing as he stared down at his fingers that were now heavily stained with blood.

"How much blood loss can a powerless Sentinel sustain before he can't go any further?" Hunter wondered aloud, angry that he was stuck here. Shit, he was angry all the time. It was a normal state of being for him, but he was even more irate and irritated than his usual pissed-off self.

Kill. Kill. Kill.

The slamming force of being compelled to dust Evils was worse than it had ever been. And he wasn't sure how long he could ignore it. He became more feral every moment that he wasn't lopping off the heads of the Evils.

Hunter swayed as he plowed through more foliage, knowing he wasn't going to last much longer.

There was no way out.

There was no way in.

Was he going to end up stuck here forever?

Kill. Kill. Kill.

The hammering in his head turned to a loud buzz, and he stumbled over a fallen tree, landing on his knees. He could see his own blood starting to cover the ground, falling in rivulets from his broken body.

Gotta keep going. Keep moving, asshole, or you're toast. You'll be lost in this never-ending bad horror flick forever.

The thought of staying there, with hairy beasts with lethal teeth pecking at his body, nearly got him on his feet, but not quite. He stumbled again, landing in a mass of gel that he'd fought before and won. Now, he wasn't sure if he still had enough strength to get out of it this time.

"I'm not going to die this way," he growled, wondering if he'd really ever die, or just live in this continual nightmare. He was immortal. Or was he human again?

Hunter fought the deathtrap he was mired in, but eventually lost the fight, sinking into darkness as the clear gel turned red from his blood.

-The End-

Read Hunter's book, A Dangerous Fury,
book 3 in The Sentinel Demon series, coming soon.

Other books in this series:
A Dangerous Bargain

For updates:
Please visit me at: http://www.facebook.com/authorjsscott
You can write to me at jsscott_author@hotmail.com
You can also tweet @AuthorJSScott

http://www.authorjsscott.com

Made in the USA
San Bernardino, CA
26 August 2016